BACKWARD GLANCES

Published by Caxton Park

Copyright © 2018 S M Dooks

All rights reserved.

S M Dooks has asserted her right
under the Copyright, Designs and Patents Act 1988
to be identified as the author of this work.

ISBN 978-1-73081-567-6

Also available as a Kindle ebook
ISBN 978-1-84396-521-3

This is a work of fiction.
Any resemblance in this novel to
persons living or dead or to
actual events is wholly coincidental.

A catalogue record for this
book is available from the British Library
and the American Library of Congress

Pre-press production
eBook Versions
27 Old Gloucester Street
London WC1N 3AX
www.ebookversions.com

Also by S M Dooks

The English Girls
L'Hermitage

For Charles Bell

BACKWARD GLANCES

S M Dooks

CAXTON PARK

Janus am I; oldest of potentates!
Forward I look and backward and below
I count as god of avenues and gates.
The years that through my portals
come and go.

Henry Wadsworth Longfellow,
written for the *Children's Almanac*.

Part One

I. Maggie

The phone call came a few days after the letter. Maggie didn't answer it because she was out with the dog, but there was a message, bleeping at her insistently, on her return. On a first hearing, it didn't seem to make any sense at all, and she wondered whether the speaker had got the wrong number. She couldn't recall a David in her immediate acquaintance, and she knew it would be some minutes before the computer in her head began to search more widely through that long list of names still stored, although temporarily forgotten. Intrigued, and perhaps even a little irritated, by this second intrusion into the steady peace of an increasingly uneventful life, she played the message again.

A strange conviction, appearing out of nowhere, that somehow the letter and the phone call were connected, made her listen much more carefully for clues, which would slot this particular message into its rightful place. The speaker was hesitant, obviously unhappy or nervous at being denied the warmth of an immediate human response. He also seemed unprepared in what he wanted to say, vital bits of information being left out altogether.

'It's David here—I wondered if we could meet before I go

to France—we need to talk about my father, there are so many blanks to be filled—I'll ring again—.'

Even though the message finished at this point, Maggie sensed the speaker was still there, uncertain, or perhaps reluctant to break the connection he had just made. She waited for the final click, and it was more than a minute before it came.

France was the clue she had been listening for, and like a sleepwalker, she returned to the kitchen, and picked up the letter she hadn't opened until yesterday morning. Suddenly the French stamp, and its smudged postmark, became even more weighted with a past which seemed determined not to recede as it should. Instead, both the letter and the phone call, were forcing her to contemplate a life she thought she had finished with, and she felt a rising resentment at such an unexpected intrusion.

Following Tom's fatal heart attack, less than a year after her own premature retirement, Maggie had made a conscious decision to let go of most of the ties which bound her to the past. She still had the boys, of course, but school, a lifelong devotion to teaching, could go. She had given it her soul for far too long, it was time to claw back something for herself. And for over fifteen years she had done just that and now, within the space of a week, a letter and a phone call had begun to dismantle her carefully constructed retreat. A familiar sense of vulnerability, buried but not gone, made her feel a lot older than her seventy three years, and she drew back instinctively, and a little angrily, from the choices she felt she was being compelled to make.

Now that David had been placed, everything else became clear, even predictable. Although it was just over a year since his father's death in a kayaking accident in France, the news had obviously only just reached him too. Perhaps he was in England to visit his father's family before going to France. That would make sense. Rosalind had mentioned in her letter, the letter Maggie was still holding, that attempts had been made to reach David through the Italian police, although with no apparent success. Obviously that situation had now changed, and David was still struggling to come to terms with his father's death. In such circumstances, a hesitant phone call to a stranger, made much more sense and Maggie felt a sharp pang of compassion for the grieving young man. She had never met him, but she felt she knew him, or at least the boy he once was seventeen years ago. When the raw pain of estrangement from his son, had made Matthew turn to Maggie for comfort and sympathy, she had heard so much about the boy he had lost, that David had become almost as real a presence to her as her own two sons. During her last years as Head of English at Layters Girls School, Matthew was an indispensable member of her department, their mutual dependence developing into a bond which was more than just professional. With the perspective of age, Maggie realised the danger of such closeness, although at the time her affection for the young teacher had seemed perfectly natural, and certainly acceptable.

Now Matthew's son was trying to get in touch with her, as well as with his father's lover Rosalind. Maggie sighed. Any venture into the past was certain to make life more complicated, and complications in human relationships was something she had striven to avoid since Tom's death. Life was manageable, if it could be kept simple. She no longer had the appetite or the energy for the maelstrom of other people's feelings, and yet, once again, she felt herself in danger of being engulfed by a tide of emotion she would be unable to control.

Since her last year at Layters Girls School, when her whole professional life had been compromised by Matthew's reckless affair with his sixth form student, Rosalind Dane, she had learnt to be very cautious about the danger inherent in all highly charged relationships. Such danger was contagious and unpredictable, and invariably rendered vulnerable and powerless all those it touched. David was an innocent, of course, and she no longer had a life which could be easily compromised, but nevertheless her whole body ached with a hesitant tension as she stood in the middle of the kitchen, the letter clutched tightly in her hand.

It is an obvious, but not always acknowledged truth, that the loss which death brings is felt differently at different times. For over fifteen years Maggie had been adjusting to such shocks, as the hammer blows of grief gradually fell more lightly, even if they would never completely disappear. Now it was the sounding board she was missing. Tom had been so good at that. Patience, born of years listening to the expression of pain, sometimes trying to track the underlying, unspoken story, had made him a natural listener, firm but not judgemental, whenever a response was called for. Maggie had often wished she had had the skill to return the favour, but she hadn't Tom's patience with the trivial and the incoherent, and he often retreated in the face of her determination to sort things out. He put it down to her being a teacher, and the need to establish order, as quickly as possible, to take control. Since her retirement and Tom's death, taking control had become even more necessary, although increasingly more difficult, as the years passed. Maggie needed a sounding board, even if she took no notice of it. In the first stage of her bereavement, she tried to imagine Tom was still there, fashioning his typical response herself, when a decision had to be made or a dilemma resolved. It had helped to begin with, that sleight of mind, which for a few moments would lull her into a false sense of reality. Now it was more difficult, Tom's absence a dark emptiness, which couldn't be imagined away. She could still guess what his response might be, but she knew it was her guess, and the only sounding board was the one which was to be found in her own head.

The letter perhaps demanded a reply, and there was an address now to write to.

The phone call, however, asked nothing of her at the moment. She couldn't return the call as David had left no number, and she refused to take any steps herself to retrieve it. She had always worked on the principle that if someone really wanted to contact you they would try again. She was prepared to wait, although it made her uneasy.

She put down the letter and switched on the kettle. She felt impatient with her own uncertainty of response, and needed to bustle about. She opened a tin of meat and crossed to the back door to fetch the dog's dish. A greedy cocker spaniel, he always insisted in chasing it into any convenient corner, in order to lick up every last morsel.

On this occasion, she was so preoccupied with her thoughts, she gave him far too much food, and as she put the dish down he looked at her with bemused pleasure, before burying his nose in the sticky mess.

A few minutes later the phone rang again, and she reached to pick it up.

II. David.

Fairview itself was what he had expected. His meeting with his grandfather wasn't. Not that his expectations had ever been clear, but they had certainly not included the abrasive distress which occurred. For the last five years he had known about the dementia, his Italian grandparents had made sure of that, but not its nature or extent. He had made some attempt to research the condition, during his flight from Rome the previous week, but its complexity and variety had overwhelmed him. The more he read, the more nervous and upset he became, and he knew that in this instance knowledge wasn't helping. The one piece of information that had been useful, was that every case was different, and individuals brought their own peculiar quirks of character to the condition.

David had only ever met his paternal grandparents a few times, and the last time had been nearly ten years ago, when he was fifteen. James and Helen, he had only ever known them by their Christian names, had called in once or twice at the villa in Tivoli, some thirty kilometres north east of Rome, when they had been touring in Italy. They had usually only stayed a night or two, just long enough to take their stranger of a grandson out for the day, but not long enough to establish them in his heart as people he could love.

The last occasion had come after a three year gap, when he had changed from boy into man. He could still recall the look of surprise, almost indignation, on their faces when he returned from town late one afternoon to find them already sipping Chianti on the terrace. It was almost as if they expected him to remain a boy for ever, and half resented the young man he had become. At the time it was a fleeting impression, soon masked by the usual warmth of greeting and eagerness to reinstate themselves as important figures in his life. Looking back, that look had taken on greater significance, and he wondered now if they had at last realised the nature of their loss, and were struggling to resist it. As far as he could remember, they didn't even stay the night on that occasion, despite earnest invitations from his grandparents to do so. They had booked a hotel in Rome, they were meeting friends there, it wasn't possible on this trip. Another time perhaps. They would be in touch. But they weren't. After that hot afternoon on the terrace, full of unexpressed tension and sense of loss, there was a long silence. It was broken eventually by the news in a letter from Helen's sister, Imogen, that Helen had developed breast cancer, and James was suffering in the early stages of dementia. David was in his second year at Bologna University, studying Italian art and literature, and the news came from a world he had never known and nearly forgotten about. He tried to feel concern when his grandfather rang to tell him, but, in truth, the words barely touched him, and for that he did feel guilt and sadness.

The reception area was airy and comfortable, and the two young women at the desk bright and welcoming. Nevertheless, David felt a certain misgiving in the face of such determined cheerfulness, as if he was being emotionally braced for what was to come.

'I'm here to see James Farr, my grandfather,' he added almost apologetically.

'Yes, we have a note of it here,' one of the young women replied smiling. 'You rang this morning I believe. We told him you were coming. Follow me.'

She headed towards some double doors to the left of the desk, and punched in four numbers on the code pad. Another set of swing doors followed, and then David found himself in a large room, liberally scattered with easy chairs and a number of rectangular tables, with easy-clean, Formica tops. A television blared too loudly from one corner, and a strong odour of cooked vegetables, beneath which a faint scent of urine could be detected, hung in the thick air. David felt an instinctive reluctance to draw breath, and looked around rather desperately for an open window. All were tightly shut, however, as if any slight breeze might be too much for the room's fragile occupants. Some seemed to be dozing, chins sunk into chests, in the easy chairs, whilst a small group was sitting at one of the rectangular tables, and appeared to be involved in some sort of game.

'I'm not fucking going there. It's the wrong end of the ship. And they've got guns.'

A white-haired woman, in a bright blue cardigan, had stood up suddenly from the table, fanning her face frantically, as if tormented by some persistent insect. A care worker, who had just entered from a door at the far end of the room, moved swiftly to pick up the overturned chair and laid a restraining hand on the woman's arm. A subdued, resentful, muttering came from the rest of the residents around the table as the woman in the blue cardigan resumed her seat, the care worker hovering anxiously at her shoulder, until the game restarted.

'What are they playing?' He asked the receptionist who was accompanying him.

'Oh only Ludo or Snakes and Ladders,' she replied brusquely. 'Anything more taxing is beyond most of them and then terrible arguments break out.'

She opened a door on the opposite side of the room from where they had entered, and ushered David into a broad corridor, from which doors led off into large, comfortable, rooms, with their own television and small bathroom. At this time of day all the doors stood open, and as far as David could see they were all empty.

'Your grandfather likes to keep himself to himself,' his companion said as she knocked on the door of one of the rooms on the left of the corridor. 'If he isn't in his room I expect he'll be in the quiet area round the corner.'

The room was empty, and as they reached the end of the corridor and turned to the left, David suddenly felt nervous and full of misgiving about the whole venture. What was he doing here? Why had he come? His grandfather, after all, was now almost a complete stranger to him, and although he remembered vividly James and Helen's infrequent visits to the villa, he had never felt close to them. He had always resisted any attempt to be drawn into his father's family, and he knew both James and Helen had been hurt by his resistance. A deep sense of anger and betrayal at his father's absence had hardened his heart, however, and from an early age he could not forgive their seeming inability to bring his father back to him. Now, news of his father's death had made it necessary to resolve things one way or another. His grandfather was old and ill, and he was determined to respond to any sign of affection which might be shown.

At first glance, the quiet area appeared to be empty too.

Four or five high backed chairs were grouped around a low coffee table, and in the far corner a large fish tank was perched on top of a specially constructed stand, where slowly changing coloured lights, provided an exotic background for the darting fish.

'Mr Farr, are you hiding again?'

The young woman was in the centre of the ring of chairs and smiled encouragingly at David over the top of the nearest one.

'You're the lucky one today. You have a visitor,' she continued. 'Do you remember we told you this morning that your grandson was coming?'

There was a reply but he couldn't make it out. The receptionist beckoned him forward, and he squeezed between two of the heavy chairs, in one of which his grandfather crouched, as if still reluctant to advertise his whereabouts.

' Hello James,' he said, extending his hand. 'It's good to see you.'

'Who are you? What do you want?'

The voice was low, but the words were clipped and angry.

'I'm David, your grandson, Matthew's son. You visited me in Italy. Do you remember?'

David's hand dropped to his side when James refused to offer his, and instead he pushed one of the chairs a little closer to his grandfather's, and sat down. 'Is Matthew here too? It's time he came to see me. His mother keeps on about it every day. I could wring that boy's neck for all the trouble he causes. Where's he got to? Has he left early? They won't let him out if he doesn't know the time.'

'James, my father, your son Matthew, is dead. He died in a boating accident in France over a year ago. You were told at the time.'

David felt a note of desperation begin to creep into his voice, and he tried to calm himself. He mustn't expect too much. His grandfather was ill, his dementia was obviously getting worse. Things were slipping away. That was what happened. He could cope with that. It was the anger he found more difficult, and the lack of recognition. That hurt the most, although he knew he was being unreasonable. It was a major part of the illness. Losing your grip on identity—your own and that of others.

'Matthew is here. He'll be back in a minute. Who are you?'

James was talking again in his quiet voice, cold as daggers, and fierce with mistrust.

'I'm David, your grandson. Matthew, your son, is my father. I wanted to see you. I'm going to France to see where he died. I thought you ought to know.'

'France? My son went to France. We lost him but he's back now. Where is he? What's he doing?'

James peered round the side of the chair impatiently, his shrunken body uncurling a little with the effort. When he turned back he gazed fixedly at David, as if seeing him for the first time.

'Are you going? I don't want you here. My son will be back in a minute. He's paying the bill. The holiday's over now.'

David winced at the hostility in his grandfather's voice, as if he had received a physical blow. He felt increasingly powerless in the face of such resistance, willed or otherwise. It had been a mistake to come. If his grandfather had ever accepted his son's death, he had forgotten it now. His mind was searching back for the comfort of the past, and David realised that any attempt to bring him into the present would only increase his anger and fear.

'It's been good to see you James,' David said as cheerfully as he could, pushing his chair back a little so he could get up. 'I have to go now.'

His grandfather raised his head, and gazed at him. David started. The cold hostility had disappeared from his grandfather's eyes, and instead a look of puzzled affection had taken its place.

'Have you come straight from school? Was I right? Was it Hamlet? Where's Helen? Where's your mother?'

David went cold inside. His grandfather had drifted even further back, avoiding the recent past, and looking for the boy he had lost. David guessed that his appearance, his voice, his gestures perhaps, had recalled something of his father, and James had seized on the likeness, as a glimpse of clarity in a world of confusion.

In his hurt, David felt tempted to shatter his grandfather's illusions and cast him back into his twilight world of bewilderment and fear.

He opened his mouth to kill his father again, but different words came.

'I've had a good day Dad. Mother's on her way.'

James nodded and reached out his hand. David grasped it sadly. It was obvious he no longer existed for his grandfather, who had thoughts only for a son now dead. David's family had shrunk a little more and he felt terribly alone.

On the way out, David noticed that the woman in the blue cardigan was no longer sitting at the table with the others. She had pulled a chair round so that she was facing the wall, and appeared to be asleep. He pressed the bell to be let out, and as he did so a string of expletives rose from the chair, and pursued him, like the Furies into the corridor and across the reception area. He barely registered the receptionist's smile and polite enquiry about his visit, before the front door swung open, and he was in the fresh air at last.

III. Maria

She could hear the boy even before she opened her eyes. His high pitched voice clung to the edge of her dream, as it slipped away like an elusive guest, and she struggled into wakefulness. And it was a struggle, every day a little harder, the heat draining her of the energy she needed to fight the slide into darkness. It would be breath-catching hot, she knew that already. The boy always rose early on the hottest days to join his grandfather for breakfast. That explained the excitement in his voice, which drifted through her window, the words lost on the way. The excitement was shriller than usual because the boy would be six in two days' time, and a special picnic was planned. It had been her mother's idea, and she felt a stirring of resentment that the boy had seized on it with such enthusiasm. Surely it was for her to plan the treats, and she had meant to. It was just that the days slipped away, until there was no time left, and her mother had to step in and promise the child something. A picnic by the lake, swimming, a boat trip, they were all to be included, and she shuddered at the thought of all that glare and heat. In the cool darkness, she could just about hang on, but in the heat and light she felt stripped bare, her raw pain exposed for all to see.

A door banged, footsteps on the stairs, and she opened her eyes. For a moment she thought he was going to come in, but the footsteps hesitated for only a moment outside her door, and then moved on and up another flight, to her parents' bedroom.

They would leave her alone for a bit, but not for long. The doctor had said she should be encouraged to get up at a normal hour and keep active. The opportunity to brood must be kept to a minimum, if she was to make progress. Progress. What did they mean by progress? The very word made her feel tired, and she shut her eyes again, as a shaft of hot sunlight from the half opened shutters, fell across the bed. Her mother would bang on the door on her way down to breakfast, but the boy wouldn't. He would be there, close behind his grandmother, but he wouldn't come in, not even if she called out to him. It stung, the pain of his rejection, but there was nothing she could do. Ever since the last episode, fear had taken over from love, and now, like a timid animal, he shrank from her presence, as if uncertain, even fearful, of what she might do next. She would have liked to have got involved in the picnic, the preparations, the excitement, the anticipation. Even as a young child, it was the thought of something, not the thing itself, which had thrilled her the most. The excitement lay in knowing it was out of sight, but still there, waiting for her. Christmas had been like that, and birthdays, and the first day of a special journey somewhere. The actual event was often a disappointment, a slow leeching of excitement, until all that was left was boredom and frustration, but the anticipation that was different, and had all the sharpness of a pleasure just waiting to be fulfilled.

There would be another episode, she knew that, but not when. The doctor also wouldn't commit himself. 'It is important to avoid the triggers,' he said as if somehow she had a choice in the matter. But she didn't. The darkness always came out of nothing, like a tsunami, breaking on the shore of her mind, and filling every indentation of her brain with a swirling debris, which left its own reeking residue as the darkness drained away. 'Also try to avoid too much excitement, too much stress,' he continued, as if only the tedium of a bland existence could guarantee stability. ' Here are some tablets for the worst moments, but don't take them unless you have to.' Always the implication that she had some control when she knew she hadn't. It was like throwing someone a life belt when they were already unconscious and drowning, she reflected bitterly. Everything was an irrelevance when the moment came, except for that tiny, hard knot of self which had, until now, refused to be swept away.

She had drifted off to sleep again before the knock came, but she could sense her mother's irritation, perhaps anxiety, in the persistent hammering on the door, which eventually penetrated her consciousness.

'It's all right I hear you,' she replied, rather peevishly. 'I'll be down soon.'

Her mother's relief hovered for a moment in the silence outside her door, and then two pairs of footsteps continued on their way, one scampering ahead of the other, now the dreaded moment had passed.

Dressing carelessly and quickly, she slipped down the stairs herself a few minutes later, gliding past the door to the kitchen, where her son's lively chatter had resumed over his cereal bowl, and out into the relative cool of the early morning garden. It was still a sanctuary at this time of the day, pools of damp shade lingering until burnt away by the sun, as it rose higher in the sky, leaving no retreat untouched.

The villa was one of a number of villas, dotted over a south west facing slope, which looked towards Rome, some thirty kilometres away. The garden was terraced to make the most of the steep slope, and was bounded by a low, stone, wall, from which there were wide views over the Roman Campagna. In the early morning, details of this expansive landscape could be picked out clearly, but as the day drew on, and the heat intensified, colours began to blur and shapes dissolve, as a haze shimmered, like a veil dropped delicately across a grand stage.

For the moment, Maria's edges felt sharp and clear, as if the coolness was holding her together. She made her way quickly down the garden towards the low, stone, wall, a sudden burst of energy making her step light and buoyant on the shallow, stone, steps which divided the garden almost equally in half. Later in the day, with the sun full on them, these steps would simmer with heat. She could remember, as a small girl, burning the backs of her legs quite badly, when, late in the day, she had sat on one of the lowest and most exposed of the steps, to watch for a lizard she had seen darting into a crack at the side of the path. So intent was she on willing the creature out of its dark lair that she barely noticed the heat of the stone penetrating the thin cotton of her shorts, and leaving sore, red, patches, on her skinny, white, legs. It was one of those days when you could almost smell the heat as it turned ordinary objects into something alien and strangely threatening. As a child, such hints of danger were part of the fascination of summer, and made her wriggle with familiar excitement. It was only as she grew older, that the excitement became tinged with darkness and a creeping, suffocating, fear. She tried to explain her feelings to her mother, who also recoiled from the extreme heat of midsummer days, but even she didn't seem to understand. She wrinkled her nose in perplexity, laid a cool hand on her daughter's forehead, and suggested playing indoors for a bit until the sun went down.

Reaching the wall, she turned right, following a narrow path she herself had worn in the scrubby grass next to it. She was making for the furthermost corner of the garden where an old oleander, so large it was becoming quite leggy in places, overhung the wall, creating a shady bower of pink, tempting her into its poisonous depths. For the moment, however, there was no need to hide herself in the little den she had fashioned for herself, in the very heart of the plant, and instead she perched on the wall, where the overhanging branches of the shrub afforded a dappled shade, sufficient to ward off most of the heat from the early morning sun. The view from the wall never failed to calm and refresh her as her eyes followed the road, winding its way through the villages of the Campagna, towards the distant city, where, on a clear day, the cupola of St. Peter, could sometimes be seen, a fragile mirage of heaven on the horizon.

It was more than five years since she had been to Rome herself, her illness making an expedition of any length a fearful experience. Even on her last visit, when she still thought she was well, the sheer noise and bustle of the teeming city had grated on her raw nerves, turning her delight in the sights she had come to see, into something bitter and metallic, which lingered on her tongue, like the aftermath of a feverish cold. The pulsing heat and light of that summer visit had been manageable then, just about, now she shuddered at the mere thought of such exposure. It was better as a mirage, which could never actually be experienced, like heaven itself, with its luminous, white light, shining angels, and dazzling throne. God, what a place that would be, she thought bitterly, leaning out a little from the wall, so that she could look into the quite extensive gardens of the villa, some way below, to the west. A large swimming pool dominated one of the lower terraces of this garden, although it was hardly ever used by the middle aged couple who owned the villa. Just occasionally, in the early part of the morning, a young man in his late teens or early twenties - son, nephew, younger brother, she wasn't sure which-- would appear and disturb the glistening blue of the pool, swimming for up to an hour, although never longer, with the dedication of the professional swimmer. On the completion of a predetermined number of lengths, the young man would lift himself effortlessly out of the pool, disdaining the steps, and lie, spread out in the sun on the hot tiles, for precisely another half an hour, before disappearing into the cool quiet of the villa.

During the summer months she had become used to the young man's regular, if rather infrequent sessions in the pool, and she would hasten most mornings to her scented eyrie, eager to catch a glimpse, if he happened to appear. The excitement lay in never knowing quite when that would be, and each morning she would become a little breathless with anticipation. Soon it was the only thing which could rouse her from her bed, although in her own mind she veered away from acknowledging such dependency, slightly ashamed of her childlike obsession with a total stranger.

The Gales, quite a wealthy couple from Guildford, who had purchased the villa only three years before, had proved resistant to any overtures of friendship from Maria's parents, and so, relatively close neighbours as they were, little was really known about them. This slight element of mystery added an extra frisson to her voyeurism, and as she watched the young man pursue his dogged swimming routine, at regular intervals, through that hot summer, she felt free to indulge in a variety of romantic fantasies, which left her feeling physically disturbed, the oleander blossoms cool against her flushed cheeks. Most social occasions were also now beyond her, so there was little chance of her actually meeting the young man, bringing a welcome safety to her imaginings. The only event she had to fear for the moment was the boy's picnic, and if the young man was to appear again this morning, she might be able to blot even that torment from her mind, for a little while at least.

She peered intently at the blue square of the pool, the dappled shade from the oleander keeping her reasonably protected from the heat of the mounting sun. There was no sign of the young man, but if he didn't appear soon she would be forced to retreat into her den, from where it was much more difficult to gain a clear view of the garden below. She glanced at her watch, it was already gone nine, and usually he would have appeared by now, if he was going to. The wall was already becoming warm in the unshaded spots, and she knew she would have to move very soon. Just as she was about to abandon the wall, and push her way into the centre of the oleander, a movement in the garden below caught her eye. It was the young man with the Gales, but it didn't look as if he was going swimming on this occasion. In fact, it looked as if all three were in the middle of a heated argument. No sound reached Maria, but the body language, particularly of the young man said it all. He was obviously being backed into a corner about something and his hosts, parents, aunt, uncle, whatever they were, seemed to be putting a lot of pressure on him. Maria felt an instinctive sympathy with the young man's situation, trapped and harassed as he appeared to be. She longed to shout words of encouragement and resistance, but the distance was too great and the dumb show played on, regardless of her rapt attention. At one point they were all standing so close to the edge of the pool it looked as if the Gales might push the young man into the water themselves. But then, as suddenly as the whole scene had arisen, it seemed to evaporate, and the Gales went back into the house, leaving the young man still standing at the edge of the pool. Whatever had been said had left him in a reflective, if irritated mood, as he appeared to be stirring the water of the pool with his foot, in a rather agitated, angry, manner, and showing no desire to embark on his customary, measured, swim. Nothing much had really happened but, nevertheless, Maria felt intrigued by the sense of drama which seemed to emanate from the scene. The breaking of the young man's usual routine had a particular significance after so many weeks, and she waited eagerly to see what he would do next. Her involvement in the scene was so complete, that she had even ventured right out from the shade of the oleander, so that she could get the best possible view of what was happening in the garden below. The thought that she might be spying on a scene that was meant to be private never entered her head. After so many weeks of watching and waiting for the young man, she felt strangely proprietorial towards him, as if she had every right to know what was going on.

It was the boy's voice which broke the spell.

'Mamma! Mamma! Are you hiding?'

The words drifted down the garden towards her.

Immediately Maria moved away from the oleander, anxious to preserve its secret, even from the prying eyes of her own child. Quickly mounting the steps towards the upper terraces she met the boy half way to the house, his small face screwed up against the bright sun.

'Nonna wants you. She says you have to come now.'

'What for?' Maria replied, already alarmed by the urgency in the boy's voice.

'It's something nice,' he replied. 'Nonna said it was. Oh do come on Mamma.'

The boy was plucking at her sleeve as he spoke, an

unfamiliar sensation, as he hardly ever touched her. Mixed with this strangeness was an irritation at his bossiness, and she brushed his hand way impatiently.

'Don't do that David. You're pinching me. It hurts.'

A muttered 'sorry', and a fleeting look of contrition on the boy's face, and then he was off, racing up the rest of the garden towards the top terrace, and disappearing like a small, burrowing, animal through the sliding, lounge doors, which had been opened earlier to let in the slight, morning breeze.

Maria followed more slowly, a hard knot of anxiety gathering in the pit of her stomach. Any slight change from her usual routine unnerved her, and she was already slightly disturbed from the scene she had just witnessed in their neighbour's garden.

Her mother was in the kitchen. She had cleared away the breakfast things and was chopping vegetables for the gazpacho she often made on the hottest days. Her knife sliced through the large tomato she was holding, with the speed and precision of a doctor's scalpel, while her grandson clapped his hands in delight at her skill.

'Can I have a go, Nonna?' he said, picking up a red onion to hand to his grandmother, just as Maria entered the room.

'Not yet, Mia cara. When you are a little older. You don't want to lose those fingers do you?'

The boy screamed in horrified delight at the thought, burying his hands in his armpits for safety.

'You shouldn't frighten him, Mummia,' Maria said sharply. 'It will only give him nightmares.'

'Nonsense,' her mother replied. 'You are never too young to learn about the dangers of this world.'

'What did you want me for?' Maria asked abruptly. She would never agree with her mother about David's upbringing, although she had to admit that the boy seemed to thrive in his grandmother's company. He had disappeared as soon as using the knife was no longer an option, and she could hear him talking quietly to himself in the next room. She also felt tired. The morning had been odd, and her nerves were jangled.

'There's been a change of plan,' her mother said briskly, eyeing her daughter warily, 'to do with David's birthday treat.'

'I thought you had already settled that,' Maria said rather bitterly. 'Why the change?'

There was a pause, while her mother chopped half a cucumber and added it to the soup.

'Well, we've had an invitation and I don't think we should turn it down.'

'What invitation? We never get invitations. I can't remember the last time you and papa went out on a social visit.'

'There have been reasons for that,' her mother replied crisply, 'but on this occasion I think we should accept.'

'Why? Why should we accept?'

Maria's grumpy weariness had changed into anger and anxiety, and she almost shouted at her mother.

'Because it's from our neighbours, the Gales. I know they have tended to resist any friendly overtures in the past, but now they seem really keen to make amends and get on good terms as neighbours.'

For a few minutes Maria felt quite knocked back by her mother's words, as the image of the young man swimming filled her head. A wave of nausea swept up from the knot in her stomach, and she suddenly felt cold in the warm kitchen.

'How does this affect David's birthday treat?' She blurted out at last, avoiding her mother's eye, and clutching the edge of the table, as she fought against the blackness, threatening to descend again.

'It's for the same day, and they want to make their invitation part of the whole occasion, if we are happy to do that. They have a lovely swimming pool apparently, very shallow at one end, so great for children. They hardly use the pool themselves, only when they have visitors; they feel it is an awful waste. Hence the invitation, I suppose.'

'Surely you didn't get all this information from a written invitation?' Maria said sarcastically.

'No, of course not,' her mother replied impatiently. 'As soon as the invitation arrived I gave them a ring, and Jeannie and I had quite a long chat. They have a young relative staying with them at the moment, I believe, so it won't just be the two of them.'

'What about the boat trip and the picnic? Have they all gone by the board then?' Maria spoke quickly, trying to conceal her agitation

'Well, Jeannie said she would get a picnic together to have by the pool. And I don't think David will mind too much about the boat trip.'

'How do you know? Have you asked him?'

Maria felt surprised by the strength of her emotions, as tears pricked in her eyes, and she turned away angrily from the table.

Her mother knew the warning signs only too well. She moved the pan of Gazpacho to the stove, and washed the knife under the running tap, returning it to the knife block at the back of one of the highest cupboards. Having wiped the table, and put the remaining vegetables away, she sat down quietly by her daughter, and put a reassuring arm round her shoulders.

'Of course we will talk to him about it. But children of his age are very adaptable. As long as they are the centre of attention, any treat will be fun. After all, he's been to the lake and on the boat many times. This will be something different; a new place, new people. It will be good for all of us'

She spoke quietly but firmly, sensing the tension beginning to drain away from her daughter's taut shoulders. She half expected a desperate plea from her daughter to be excused the occasion, but strangely there was none. Perhaps it would come later, when the full implication of what such a visit would entail really hit her. In the meantime, her job was to ward off the demons as best she could. She sighed. It wasn't going to be easy.

IV. Matthew

Matthew had never meant to run away with one of his students. What teacher would, unless he or she was determined on professional suicide? When he joined Maggie Pool's English Department at Layters School, he was a young man full of ambition to go to the very top of his profession. His knowledge and enthusiasm had impressed Maggie from the start, and she was delighted to welcome such an outstanding teacher to her department. It wasn't long before they both realised that they shared the same view of education, its purpose and practice. The ability to create a passion for English Literature in their students was of the upmost importance to both of them, and something at which they both excelled. Matthew was convinced he had found the English Department, where he would be allowed to flourish in his own way, and very soon a close bond had been established between Head of Department and aspiring, young, teacher.

From his first day at the school, Matthew made a point of getting in early every morning, and as Maggie was always early too, they quickly fell into the habit of sharing ideas, problems, and successes over a cup of coffee in the staff room, before any other members of the department arrived. Most of their discussions were about professional matters, but as time went on, and they came to know each other better, personal things began to creep into their conversations as well. By the end of his first term at the school, Matthew had told Maggie something of his ill-fated affair with Maria, a fellow student at Durham. He didn't go into a lot of detail but she knew that the girl became pregnant during their second year, and that he was put under a lot of pressure from her parents to marry her. The marriage duly took place, Matthew returned to his studies, and Maria was whisked off to Italy after the baby was born, for an extended holiday, her father was Italian, and that effectively was the end of the relationship. A couple of years later Maria's parents moved out to live permanently in Italy, taking their daughter and grandson with them, and as far as Maggie could tell, Matthew hadn't seen the boy since.

Matthew seemed happy for Maggie to know this much, but was very resistant to any probing about his feelings, now that both wife and child appeared lost to him. Matthew found it hard to explain such reticence, even to himself, as he had complete trust in Maggie's discretion, and knew that she would listen with genuine sympathy to any explanation of his tangled emotions about the whole affair. The trouble was he barely understood the feelings himself; to articulate them with any clarity to another was impossible. He was fairly clear about his feelings for Maria, it was his feelings about the boy which caused the problem. The intense love, romantic yet lustful, which he had felt for Maria didn't survive the marriage but withered away in the face of parental concern, and the prospect of fatherhood. He was only nineteen, and suddenly the world seemed to be closing in on him, shutting down his options, and handing the control to others.

He saw nothing of Maria during the last months of her pregnancy, her parents forbad it, and his own were also anxious that he detach himself from the whole business as soon as possible. The fact that he was now married to Maria seemed to be regarded as nothing, but a nod to decency, by everyone else, and not something which entitled him to have any say in the matter. The day the boy was born, Maria's parents did have the grace to ring him, and a visit was arranged for the following day. Matthew could still remember all the details of that day, with an aching clarity, which most of the time he worked hard to suppress.

The name, David, had been decided on by both of them soon after Maria first realised she was pregnant, and so there was no decision to be made there.

That was very fortunate, it turned out, as Maria didn't want to see him when he arrived at the hospital, laden with an expensive bunch of red roses he couldn't really afford, and a whole assortment of soft toys for the baby. She was tired, he was informed, and probably suffering from post-natal depression, so would he mind just seeing the baby. The nurse was friendly and cheerful, but looked at him rather anxiously, as she gave him this news, as if expecting an indignant outburst and a demand to be allowed to see his wife. Instead, Matthew nodded his head in quiet agreement with the change of plan, secretly relieved that the awkwardness of such a meeting had been removed.

He was shown into a small side ward, where David had been brought straight from his mother's bedside. He had just been fed and his tiny mouth was still making little sucking movements, as if hopeful of a return to the breast. For a few moments Matthew stared in disbelief at this scrap of humanity he had fathered, waiting for the emotional link which would confirm his connection with his son.

The baby had dark hair, like his father, and piercing blue eyes, which the young nurse told him would most likely change. His skin, slightly tinged with yellow from neo-natal jaundice, was smooth and firm, and there were no ugly red blotches, common to the new born. The child was beautiful and Matthew couldn't take his eyes off him. An almost uncontrollable desire to snatch up the child and carry him off, rolled over him, and he found himself shaking with the emotional turmoil it left behind. A reassuring hand on his arm brought the tears to his eyes, and he brushed them away quickly, embarrassed and confused by his own weakness.

'You can pick him up and give him a cuddle,' the young nurse said, her voice coming as if from a great distance, ' he won't break you know. You'd be surprised how strong new born babies can be.'

Matthew leant over the cot and picked up his son.

Even telling Maggie the bare facts was hard enough. It brought back all the raw emotion, and sense of loss, he had been trying to come to terms with over the last few years. Teaching, the job at Layters, and the support of such a good Head of Department as Maggie, had helped of course. The feelings he might have had for a wife and child were transformed into an even greater passion for the subject he loved, as he struggled to adapt to the reality of his situation. The feelings he tried to suppress were not all negative ones, however. The joy at having fathered a child remained, even if buried under the deadening weight of grief and regret. He had assumed, that even if everything was over between Maria and himself, he would still be able to see David, and not long after that first visit to the hospital, he wrote to Maria's parents, asking if a formal arrangement could be made, regarding when and how often he could see his son. The reply was civil but cool. He wasn't exactly refused access, that wouldn't be allowed, but he was actively discouraged from taking the matter any further. He knew he would be in for a fight if he wanted to play a significant role in his son's life, and for a time grief and anger gave him the strength to resist the efforts which were being made to separate him from David. With the help of the university's legal department, and the students' union, he engaged a lawyer, but soon realised he wouldn't be able to meet the costs without some help from his parents. He approached them reluctantly, and although they were prepared to pay his legal bills for a time, they were not prepared for a long, drawn- out, battle through the courts. In many ways he was not in a strong position, or that is how it seemed to him at the time. He was very young, a penniless student, and what is more Maria refused to have anything to do with him, becoming hysterical and even violent, if it was suggested that they should meet and discuss the situation. Even her parents seemed upset and embarrassed by her extreme reaction, and despite their wish to keep Matthew apart from the child, if at all possible, they nevertheless, felt obliged to let him see the boy occasionally. As a result, Matthew was given the opportunity to see David perhaps six or seven times during the first two years of his son's life. The visits were carefully managed by Maria's parents, Matthew usually meeting David with the au pair, who had been hired to look after him, in a local park, close to Maria's parents' house, on the outskirts of York. Difficult as it was sometimes for Matthew to make these visits, as they were often arranged, perhaps deliberately, at very short notice, he never failed to turn up. Such infrequent meetings made it hard for a real bond to be created between father and son, but Matthew hoped that if he could just keep the connection alive, one day things might change, and he would be in a position to play a proper role in his son's life.

A change did come about but not the one Matthew had anticipated and hoped for. One morning in June, two weeks after he had last seen David, and when he was coming to the end of his PGCE year, which he had elected to do in York to be nearer to his son, a letter arrived at his rather grubby digs near Bootham Bar.

Matthew recognised the handwriting as that of his parents-in-law, and immediately felt a sense of alarm. Another meeting with David wasn't to be arranged for several weeks, and anyway these communications were always by email, never letter.

Looking at the letter more closely, his alarm deepened. The stamp was Italian and the postmark Roma.

Ripping open the envelope, his worst fears were confirmed, and with them a dreadful sense of the inevitable. Maria and her parents had moved to Italy permanently, and they had taken David with them. Maria was unwell, no more details were given, and her parents were planning to apply for legal guardianship of David themselves through the Italian courts. Matthew was strongly advised not to pursue the matter any further. If he did so the cost could be prohibitive.

During the last few weeks of his PGCE course, Matthew lived in a daze of grief, bewilderment, anger, and despair. His heart ached with a sense of loss, strangely detached from David himself, although any glimpse of a pushchair or a toddler's faltering steps, sent a sick shudder through his whole body, and he turned away quickly to blot out the image. He was still angry, but Matthew knew he wouldn't fight it any more. He was too young, too overwhelmed by the resistance ranged against him, and finally too exhausted emotionally to cope. The feeling that he had betrayed David, abandoned him too easily, lingered like a persistent toothache, blotting out all other pain in its quivering intensity.

Relief, if not salvation, came through his work. He knew he was lucky to get the job at Layters, a well-known girls' grammar school in the south of England, and from his very first day in Maggie's department, he threw himself into the job, with all the passion and energy of a man who was determined to move on. He had always been able to immerse himself totally in the Literature he was studying for his degree, now he could do the same with all the books he had to teach from year 7 upwards. In every lesson, he was like a coiled spring, taut with enthusiasm and excitement, for all he had to teach, and it wasn't long before he was one of the most popular teachers in the English Department. He also made a great impression on Maggie, who in the last decade of her teaching career, relished the young man's intellectual edge and challenging presence in the department.

'You are going to stir us all up,' she said to him laughing, during one of their early- morning meetings, not long after he had joined the school. 'The girls will hang on your every word. Be careful. That is a great responsibility to carry.'

Matthew smiled. He felt so grateful for the encouragement and support. The healing had begun.

Rosalind had first come to Matthew's notice in the autumn term of 2011, when he took over a year 11 group from Maggie. The senior management of the school had decided that Heads of the biggest departments in the school, such as English, Maths and Science, needed more non-contact time, and as Maggie was teaching two year 11 groups, she decided to relinquish one to Matthew's tender care.

'Look after them,' she said firmly to the young man. 'There's quite a mixture of ability, but they are a good group overall. I feel I am letting them down a bit, handing them over to someone else mid-course, but I am sure they will all do well, with the right support and guidance.'

'I'll do my best,' Matthew replied with equal seriousness, 'and I hope I can encourage quite a few to continue their study of English Literature into the sixth form.'

'That's great,' said Maggie, pleased by such a positive response. 'I have already earmarked one or two of the girls as possible English graduates of the future. Rosalind Dane stands out particularly in that respect.'

It wasn't surprising, therefore, that from the first lesson he took with his new year 11 group, Matthew was keen to identify and get to know the very promising student, who had already caught the notice of his highly experienced Head of Department. He wasn't disappointed. From the outset, Rosalind's liveliness, her intellectual verve and her challenging response to all the Literature they were studying, ensured that she was the catalyst for some very productive discussion in the group as a whole. It wasn't long before he realised that he was coming to rely on her contribution to keep the lessons moving. Conscious that such reliance might be construed as favouritism, he made a special effort to focus more specifically on other members of the group. As a result, discussions tended to lose some of their edge, and Matthew sensed that Rosalind was a little affronted, if not quite upset, by the way she was being deliberately marginalised by the teacher who had responded so enthusiastically to her ideas during the first few weeks of term.

One Friday, just before half term, Rosalind hung back after the lesson, as if anxious to have a word with Matthew. It was the last lesson of the afternoon and all the other girls left the classroom very quickly, their minds already on their plans for the weekend, as thoughts about Macbeth were put away for another week.

Sifting through the essays which had just been handed in, Matthew was acutely aware of the girl, hovering at the edge of his vision, and he waited a little apprehensively for her to speak. He guessed that she might want to complain about being ignored, and he tried to formulate a response in his head which would explain the problem, as he saw it, but not be too discouraging. He could sense the tension in the girl, as she fiddled with the coloured stickers marking important quotations in the text, and felt obliged to try to defuse the situation.

'Did you want to see me about something, Rosalind?' He said at last, rather lamely, shoving the essays into a plastic folder, and putting them together with his computer and some spare texts, he had brought from the stock cupboard.

'No. Sorry. I should be going,' she replied abruptly, her cheeks crimson as she refused to meet his gaze.

He opened his mouth to offer some words of reassurance, but she had already turned away to put her chair on the desk, and then she was gone.

For a few moments Matthew stared at the gently swinging door, guilty and disconcerted, but uncertain why.

From then on lessons with the group assumed an importance in the week which he was unable to shrug off. On the one hand, he found himself, adolescent fashion, almost counting the minutes before the next lesson, and on the other, feeling angry with himself for allowing such feelings to dominate his thoughts, in such a ridiculous way. He even considered asking Maggie to take the group back, or swap it with a more junior one, but in the end felt too ashamed to suggest it. He despised his own weakness, depressed by the suspicion that he was falling into the oldest trap of all.

On several occasions he was on the point of telling Maggie about it in their early morning meetings, but again the thought that he might go down in her estimation as a result, was too much to bear. He was fairly certain she would be sympathetic, even supportive, on a personal level, but professionally it would inevitably cause an element of doubt, which would be hard to eradicate.

During half term, Matthew shut up his flat on the far side of town, and went home to his parents in Yorkshire. He took a lot of work with him to keep himself occupied, and when too tired to read or plan any more lessons, he went off on long walks up the dales, seeking refuge in a physical exhaustion, which left no room for undisciplined thoughts and desires.

After half term, Maggie was down to give a series of talks to the whole of year 11 about A-Level courses in English, in order to help them make the right choices. She regarded the task as so important for future recruitment of students to the department that she was never prepared to delegate it. It was essential that the information and approach was consistent in all the talks, and the tone had to be right too.

To help her enthuse potential A-Level English students, she would ask for volunteers from the year 12 and 13 groups she was already teaching, to come along and join her in the talks. She found they invariably made excellent ambassadors for the subject, and presented the students' experience of actually studying the subject in a way, which never failed to convince and excite.

In the autumn of 2011, however, she decided to change things a bit. In addition to asking for volunteers from the girls, she invited Matthew to join the team. She already knew how highly regarded he was by all his students, and it seemed a shrewd move to use his obvious success as a teacher for the benefit of the whole department. His response to the invitation, however, surprised her a little. He seemed nervous and reluctant, brushing off his popularity with the students impatiently, even angrily.

'If you are really not happy to join in we'll leave it then,' Maggie said regretfully, 'but it's a pity. I think the girls would have appreciated your input.'

She looked narrowly at Matthew, suddenly anxious that the young man wasn't settling in quite as well as she had hoped.

He made no reply, but gathered his books together, ready to leave for the first lesson as soon as the bell went.

'I am thinking of giving you a year 12 group next year,' she said, as he stood up. 'You would share it with me. I think it could work well. How do you feel about that?'

'Fine, absolutely fine,' Matthew replied quietly, 'whatever you think best.'

There was nothing to object to in such an answer but Maggie still felt strangely dissatisfied with it.

'Anyway, plenty of time to think about that in the months ahead,' she concluded brightly, as he opened the door. She didn't have time to hear if he made any reply, as the door swung quickly to behind him.

Despite feeling strongly drawn towards her, Matthew kept an appropriate professional distance from Rosalind throughout the rest of the autumn term, and well into the spring term. Preparations for the Mock examinations in December kept them all very busy, and there were fewer opportunities for open discussion as they all concentrated on the necessary revision. Matthew knew, from the detailed notes she was making, that Rosalind was working particularly hard, and whenever he took in the students' notes to check they were on the right lines, he was particularly impressed by Rosalind's, which were incisive, perceptive, and frequently very erudite. He even found himself copying down some of her observations into his own text, acknowledging his debt in a hastily written note, which he attached to her sheaf of papers, when he handed them back. Out of the corner of his eye, he saw the colour begin to rise in her face, when she spotted the note, and to save her confusion, he looked away, deliberately engaging in earnest conversation with another student who had come up to collect her notes.

Rosalind's results in the Mock examinations were outstanding, and Matthew was unable to contain his delight when he handed the papers back in January.

'This is really excellent work, Rosalind. I hope it means you will choose to study English Literature for A Level. It would be a complete waste of your remarkable talents if you don't.'

For a few moments the girl looked directly at Matthew, and he saw that her eyes were full of tears.

'Please, don't get upset,' he said more quietly, dropping his voice so that no other girls could hear. 'If you want to come and talk over your choices more privately, come and see me after school today. I'll be here until five.'

A brief nod of acknowledgement or acceptance, and the whole incident was over. No-one had noticed anything, but Matthew felt instinctively that something momentous had happened. He also knew, without any doubt, that it wouldn't end well, and yet he had to go on. What he was feeling was wrong, and what he might do would be even worse. He could see with a startling clarity all the consequences of his actions, but that still didn't change a thing. He knew he would be in that classroom until five.

The choice lay with Rosalind now.

She did turn up. He knew she would, and almost a year later they ran away together to France. What went on between these two events was complicated. In the eyes of many it would probably be deemed criminal, despite the fact that Rosalind was over sixteen before there was any suggestion of a relationship between them. It was certainly unprofessional, a blatant betrayal of trust, although Rosalind herself could never be persuaded to see it that way.

'It was my own decision, there was no pressure at all from you,' she said to Matthew years later, on one of the many occasions, when they returned to prod at the agonising sense of guilt he still had about the whole affair. 'In fact quite the opposite,' she continued, as they gazed out from a viewing point at the top of the gorge, over the village nestling in its depths, which they had made their home. 'You tried to break it off several times. Surely you remember the Bronte trip? The walk to Wuthering Heights—and Maggie?'

She trailed to a halt, uncomfortable memories making them both blush, like self- conscious teenagers.

'Of course,' he replied softly. 'I shall never forget that day. Something was set in motion then which still isn't finished today.'

'Our love, you mean,' she said, almost gaily, pressing his hand against her cheek.

'Yes, that, ' he was still speaking softly and she strained to catch his words. 'But there were, are,' he corrected himself quickly, 'also consequences, and I don't think they've run their course yet by any means.'

'What are you talking about?' Rosalind asked, a little alarmed by the seriousness of his tone.

'Well, for one thing,' he said slowly, trying to put thoughts he had never really formulated clearly, even to himself, into words which wouldn't sound too trite or neurotic, 'there will come a day when people will want to know more, have some sort of explanation, confront us face to face over the whole business.'

'What people? Who are you talking about?' Rosalind said, her alarm rapidly turning to irritation with Matthew's rather deliberate vagueness.

'David, my son David for one,' Matthew retorted, with uncharacteristic sharpness, 'whom I haven't seen since he was two years old. The absentee father with a vengeance,' he added bitterly.

Rosalind held his hand tightly, feeling his pain on her pulse as she always did, whenever he mentioned David. There was nothing she could say to defuse the pain- she knew that. All she could do was feel it with him, and wait for the worst to pass. Usually the mention of David brought any talk between them to an abrupt end, but not this time.

'And then there are our parents whom we've sidelined, marginalised, deliberately left out-- put it how you like- but one day somebody will have to say something.

There are too many loose ends, it's not fair on anybody. There's Maggie too. What do we do about Maggie? We put her in an impossible position.'

He wasn't speaking bitterly anymore, just sadly, and Rosalind felt unable to say anything, her heart squeezed into a tight knot of love.

These episodes of questioning, of guilt, even of remorse, had their roots in the year in school, where every day was coloured by searing moments of joy and jealousy, fear and lust. It had been so difficult, so compromising, so wrong, and yet they had still gone on. Meetings out of school were fraught with the fear of discovery, and they went to great lengths to try to find places where they would be unlikely to be spotted by anyone from the school. On several occasions, they knew they were being a little careless, but they seemed to get away with it.

Their meetings at Matthew's flat were very few. He had not long moved into a new flat, nearer to the school, which meant that Rosalind might easily be spotted by girls or staff if she visited him there.

The risk was too great, and could only be ignored on very special occasions. One of those occasions was February 14th 2013, not many weeks before the fateful trip to Haworth. In fact, it was on that day that Matthew had first told her, in some detail, about the letter Charlotte Bronte had written to Monsieur Heger, the teacher she had fallen obsessively in love with during her time in Bruxelles. They had just made love, with an intensity of desire, which took them both by surprise, and afterwards they talked of this other love, so like their own in some respects, with an emotional recognition which neither of them could deny. From that evening, fiction and reality, the past and the present, love and rejection, became an integral part of their own relationship, and it was to reach its apotheosis, some weeks later, in rain-swept ruins high on a Yorkshire moor. Matthew knew that his memories of the trip to Haworth were distorted and unreliable. Some things had been deliberately forgotten, and others rationalised until acceptable, and he left them like that. Certain moments remained true, however, and refused to be manipulated. Among these, the expression on Maggie's face, when she discovered them making love in a dark corner of Wuthering Heights, still troubled his dreams, as did the shame and relief he had felt when Maggie had visited his room that evening, and he had broken down and told her everything. Even many years later, he would never willingly go beyond that point, although he knew Rosalind had guessed the truth.

Just once they spoke about it, skirting round the edges, with a decorum and sensitivity which they were both aware of. Matthew was grateful that Rosalind had made it so easy for him, but he could never quite get over the feeling that he had betrayed both women, in a way which shouldn't really ever be forgiven. He knew Rosalind had understood because she had loved Maggie too, and so they could share the guilt of what they had done to her. Selfish and reckless in their love, they had left Maggie in an impossible position, with no option but to retire early, a question mark still hanging over her professional integrity. Matthew always hoped that the day would come when he could give Maggie the explanation she deserved, but he never actually did anything to make it possible. The years went by, and the new life he had made with Rosalind, in a tiny village, at the bottom of a deep gorge in the Cevennes, soon became the only life he wished to acknowledge. Ties with the past had to be severed, and all the obligations that went with them. Such action was not without pain, of course, and for Matthew it centred on David and Maggie. Oddly perhaps, he never worried about his parents. They had always encouraged his independence, and the real break had been made when he left home to go to Durham. After that he only saw them intermittently, often spending university vacations with other friends and then Maria, as their affair became more serious. It didn't take much effort to persuade himself that his parents would understand, and he was prepared to settle for that.

Thoughts about Maggie and David, however, were resistant to such dismissal.

In the case of both of them, the sense of betrayal went too deep, gnawing away at Matthew's conscience, in a way which often led to short but quite severe bouts of depression. When the black mood descended, he would take his kayak and spend all day on the river, letting its ageless beauty soothe and restore. From the moment they had arrived in the village, he had loved the river, and had soon become an expert kayaker, and very knowledgeable about all aspects of the gorge. For a time, before he secured a teaching job at the secondary school, he even worked for the local kayak company, hiring out boats to visitors, and instructing them about kayaking on the river safely. Rosalind accompanied him on a few occasions, but most of her spare time was usually devoted to her writing, and he was free to explore the river and its magnificent gorge, on his own.

It wasn't long before he had some favourite spots along the river, which he would retreat to, when he felt the darkness threaten to descend, and his thoughts turned to the victims of his weakness. Matthew's love for his son changed, but didn't diminish. The close, physical bond gradually disappeared, but the aching sense of loss remained, raw and vivid, fuelled by the image of the staggering toddler playing and replaying in his head, until he could have screamed from the pain. He didn't, of course, instead he took to the water and headed down the river. Favourite among all his haunts was a spot, in the very narrowest part of the gorge, where the towering cliffs almost closed overhead, and deep, dark, pools in the river were filled with the gliding shadows of huge trout. On his right, as he let the kayak drift downstream, was a huge rock face, divided in two by a great cleft in the limestone, which widened out to form a deep cave, into which the river flowed swiftly. Over time, a small, stony beach had been created, dotted with a few scrubby bushes, and the occasional piece of driftwood, temporarily abandoned by the current, as it swept on its way.

During the summer months he would visit the spot, in the early morning or late evening, to dodge the holidaymakers, but out of season the river was very quiet, and he could be guaranteed peace and solitude, at almost any time. After several visits, he decided to make the cave a slightly more permanent base, with a few home comforts. An old picnic rug with a pvc backing, a strong torch to penetrate the darkness at the back of the cave, an airtight, plastic container to store some of his favourite biscuits, and a couple of bottles of water, were all gradually assembled, between two large rocks, which formed a natural cupboard at the side of the cave. He even left an old sweater there for when the evenings became chilly, wrapped around an Anthology of Romantic Poetry, he was studying with some of his students at the secondary school.

From May to mid-October, it was quite safe to take a kayak on the river, whereas during the winter months the river became very unpredictable, swollen with water pouring off the Causse, and flowing swiftly over treacherous stretches of submerged rocks, the strong current swirling under the overhanging rock faces, with great force. Matthew had been advised to abandon the river during those months, as it was considered too dangerous for even the most expert kayaker. He accepted his banishment rather grudgingly, but he could see how anxious Rosalind became when the days shortened, the wind picked up, and the roar of the river, as it rushed over the small weir, slightly upstream from the main part of the village, could be heard even in their flat.

It was at this time, that they both felt most isolated from all they had known in that other life. To get through these months, when the village emptied of tourists and withdrew into itself, they both threw themselves into their work. Matthew concentrated hard on new English courses for his older students, while Rosalind settled down to her writing whenever she could. Her work as a waitress in a local hotel stopped over the winter months, although she still had some secretarial work at the school to fit in, but it never amounted to more than two or three hours a day. These part time jobs had been very important when they first arrived in the village, and even after Matthew secured his teaching job, they were reluctant to give up the extra income Rosalind brought in. Matthew, nevertheless, sensed that she sometimes resented the interruptions to her writing, and as time went on, and his teaching appointment was made permanent, he urged her to give them up.

'We can manage now. My job is secure,' he said one afternoon, towards the end of August, two years after they had first arrived in the gorge. 'Chuck it all in and concentrate on your writing. Isn't that what you want?'

Rosalind nodded, grateful for his consideration, but obviously still doubtful.

'Everything is rather uncertain,' she said at last. 'I think I'll keep my options open a little longer. Anyway I don't know yet if my writing is ever going to amount to much.'

'Well, you never will know if you don't give yourself a chance,' Matthew replied smiling. 'I've got faith in you. You should have too.' Despite his encouraging words, Matthew understood her doubts, and secretly applauded her common sense in not giving up 'the day jobs' just yet. She was such a passionate, impetuous, unconventional, woman in so many ways, and he loved her for that. But underneath it all was a realist, hard-headed and practical, and he knew how much he depended on her. Sometimes, in his darkest moments, he would dare to wonder what life would be like without her, pushing his imagination so far, that his whole body ached at the thought. He knew he was foolish to anticipate something which might never happen, but from a child he had always believed that if you expected the worst, it would never happen. It was always what you hadn't expected which got you in the end.

Despite the fear and anxieties, the dark moments which sometimes threatened to overwhelm him, Matthew never once regretted running away with the student he had fallen so deeply in love with. It wasn't a self-indulgent fling, the uncontrolled impulse of a weak, selfish man, the foolishness of an immature romantic, as so many probably thought. If it had been, he would have been the first to condemn his actions. But it wasn't. It was something solid and lasting, something fine and true, to set against the dark. He knew it, and Rosalind knew it, and yes, probably, Maggie knew it too. It was enough.

V. Rosalind

Sainte.....
Gorges.....
Lozere
France
March 2030

Dear Mrs Pool,

I won't begin by saying I hope you remember me, because I know that you will. What we did was unforgivable, and our long silence about it, perhaps even more so. We owed you an explanation seventeen years ago, but despite that shabby betrayal, I hope you can accept one now.

In a few days' time, you will receive a parcel from me. It is the manuscript of the novella I have just finished writing, and it tells the story of the saint associated with the French village where Matthew and I finally went to ground so many years ago. Looking back at what I've written, I realise that the saint's story and my own have many things in common, which may help to make that unfinished story you deserve to hear, a little more understandable, and bearable.

I know this will be a shock, but the first thing I have to tell you is that Matthew is dead. I still find it so hard to write the words, but there they are, on the page, and nothing can erase their truth. It was an accident. A stupid, unnecessary, accident, which should never have happened. And it was Matthew's fault entirely. There I've said it now. It's been in my head for a year, the terrible anger, but this is the first time I've really admitted it to myself. It's easier in a letter than face to face, and because you loved him too, I think you will understand.

But I am getting too far ahead. I must go back to the beginning, and try to tell a coherent story. It is not easy to revisit a past which has led to such a devastating end, but I must do it, as much for my own sake, as for yours.

When we left England behind us in July 2013, we were two thoughtless, selfish, people, putting our own feelings before anyone else's, and we had no right to expect happiness, as the result of such a careless lack of concern for others. But we were happy, achingly so sometimes, and remained so for more than fifteen years. Don't get me wrong, we had our problems, times when we hated each other for what we had done, but through all those dark moments, neither of us ever believed we could have done anything else. We knew that everyone, although perhaps not you, would condemn us for what we had done, the temerity of such scandalous self-indulgence. It may sound strange, but the knowledge that the world was against us, both strengthened our determination to see it through, and left us prey to doubts and recriminations, which were a severe test of our love.

Matthew found it harder to carry the burden of what we had done than I did. He felt he was responsible for our life, separated from family and friends, and never fully forgave himself for that. It was nonsense of course. I was just as much to blame, more so perhaps. He tried to bring our affair to an end, but I didn't give him a chance. Even as a naive, over romantic, seventeen-year-old, I sensed his vulnerability, his still raw pain from relationships which had already failed, and I exploited it without a thought for the consequences. And one of those consequences was how the whole business would affect you, someone whose loyalty and affection, we both took advantage of. Over the years I have thought so often of the dilemma we presented you with, and how our silence must have only added to the hurt. In breaking that silence, I hope I can start to put something right.

Matthew and I loved each other very much, and we made a good life for ourselves in our remote corner of France. But actions have consequences, and there is always a price to pay in the end. It has taken me a year to accept that fact, but I think I have done so now, and there's a reason for that, which takes me back to our arrival in the village, and the beginning of our life here.

We both fell in love with the village at first sight. Travelling south through France, we had no clear idea where we would end up, although Matthew knew the region of the Cevennes mountains quite well, from previous visits as a boy, and felt sure we should find a refuge somewhere. He was right. The village, when we found it, more than fulfilled our wildest expectations. From the top of a deep gorge our gaze was drawn down, down, down, to a huddle of slate, grey, roofs, clinging to the side of the rock face, and embraced by a curve in the river, a thread of silver in the shadows.

An immediate connection seemed to be made between us and this unknown community, hidden away from the world's gaze. Of course, the reality was rather different from the romantic fantasy, but I don't think either of us ever entirely lost that sense of wonder at our first sight of the village. We immediately felt at home, even during those early, fraught, weeks. Despite our anxiety about finding suitable accommodation, and our constant fear of discovery, we were both determined to stay. And we did. Problems were resolved, friends emerged, and a routine of life established. Admittedly our income was rather precarious to begin with, but we managed. Matthew secured a seasonal job with the canoe company, based in the village, and I was offered waitressing work in the main hotel, where we stayed for a few nights, when we first arrived. Matthew loved his job, such a contrast to teaching, and right from the outset he was obsessed by the river, spending all the time he could on it or near it. At weekends, when I was attempting to write, he would take his kayak, and disappear for the whole day, as he set out to explore every twist and turn of the river and its gorge. I went with him sometimes, swept along by his enthusiasm and my love for him. He had his favourite spots along the river and was always eager to share them with me.

We knew, of course, he would have to find a more permanent and better paid job before long, and once we felt settled in the village, Matthew made a few tentative inquiries about a possible teaching post, in the local secondary school. Despite its size, the village was still able to provide both Junior and Secondary education for its children, drawing some additional pupils from other, even smaller villages, further down the gorge, or up on the Causse.

Nothing came of his inquiries for several years, but then, at last, a vacancy for an English teacher came up, and with the help of friends we had made in the village, Matthew secured the post. I believe he gave your name as a referee, but I don't think it was ever taken up. The school Management Board seemed quite happy to take him on in a temporary capacity, with few or no checks, and after he had proved himself, the position was made permanent. We were now financially secure, and although Matthew urged me to give up my part time jobs, working as a waitress and sometimes in the school office, I didn't want to. I should have loved to have devoted more time to my writing, of course, but I didn't want to lose the independence my jobs brought me. I loved Matthew very deeply, but we couldn't marry, and if he were to leave me ... I knew I shouldn't have had such thoughts, but despite all my passion and bravado, I still felt very vulnerable and very young sometimes. In most people's eyes, yours as well I suspect, I had done something very foolish and immature. During those first few weeks after we ran away, I often tried to imagine what things were being said about us, and the hurt we had caused. Shame and pride can be a toxic mix, but they buoyed me up through some difficult times, and if I'm completely honest, made it impossible for me ever to go back on anything I had done. Not that I ever wanted to, and as the years passed, I felt more and more justified in the choices I had made. We had a good life together, and it seemed to stretch ahead for years to come.

Matthew seemed happy in his teaching job, and I harboured secret hopes that one day I would see my work in print. Matthew always gave me space to be myself; it was just one of the many things I loved him for. I, in return, understood how much the river, and the solitary escape it provided, came to mean to him. He was a restless spirit, and there were demons he had to fight. He spoke very rarely of either David or Maria, but I knew when they were on his mind. It was usually during the winter months, when it was too dangerous to go on the river, and his customary means of escape was closed to him. Instead he would bury himself in his school work, or play Petanque with his friend Luc. But it wasn't enough, and although I said nothing at the time, I feared his restlessness. Matthew was never fully at peace with himself, because of what he had lost, except when he was on the river. Our love brought him great happiness, but it couldn't still his soul— only the river seemed able to do that. It was something to do with its unceasing movement, playful and exuberant, like a child during the summer months, raging and merciless, like a tyrant, during the spring and autumn rains. Matthew often spoke of the moods of the river, as if he found consolation, in its variety and unpredictability. He loved the races of wild water, when the kayak would leap and dance, with a will of its own, and he would need all his skill to guide it safely past half-submerged rocks. He also found delight in the deep, dark, pools, where the current slowed and the kayak would drift lazily above the gliding shadows of huge trout. I think he felt the river was testing him sometimes, his vigilance and skill, and he was exhilarated by the challenge. Years passed and he became an expert in reading the river, even in the dark.

At first I was terrified at the thought of him alone on the river at night, but gradually I stopped worrying, as he always returned safely, happy with the excitement of an added challenge. The nights when he had been on the river, he would often make love to me, with such passion and tenderness, as if desperate to share his joy. We were very close at those moments, although we never spoke of them. It was if any attempt to put our feelings into words would break the spell, the river and the night, had woven for us.

All very fanciful, I expect you are thinking, but don't forget we were both incurable romantics, and we never lost that. I knew that the river and the lovemaking brought Matthew the peace he longed for, even if it didn't last, and I was so glad and, yes, relieved to be part of it. I think we both felt, right from our first few days in the village, that the place, or something in the place, was healing us.

We never spoke directly of these feelings, but they were closely linked to a story we had been told, not long after our arrival. It gripped my imagination immediately, and although Matthew was more sceptical, I could tell he was still quite deeply moved by some elements in the tale. The village, our village, as we came to think of it, was named after a saint, who also found her destiny there. She wasn't a saint to begin with, of course, that came later, but she was a princess, and one with a terrible secret. In the face of an arranged marriage with a man she did not love, she begged God to save her from her terrible fate. His answer came in the form of something even more terrible, which changed the direction of her life dramatically, and for ever. She fell victim to the curse of leprosy, which drove her from her home in search of a healing spring she had been told of in a vision. That journey led to our village, where she did indeed find the cure for her affliction. The only catch was that if she attempted to leave the village and the gorge, her leprosy would return. She could only be whole if she remained. She accepted her fate, and founded an abbey in the village, which became famed throughout the region for its healing ministry.

At some point, however, our princess renounced her spiritual life as leader of the religious community she herself had founded, and retired to a cave, high up on the side of the gorge, to live the rest of her life as a recluse. Why she did this, no one knows. So many aspects of her story are shrouded in mystery, which becomes more impenetrable with time. From the moment I first heard the story, however, I could not get it out of my mind, and Matthew was certainly intrigued enough to join me on the climb to the Hermitage, a small chapel high up on the side of the gorge, which had been built out from the cave, where the Saint had supposedly lived. There was undoubtedly something unusual about the place, we both felt it. Whether this was simply the power of our own imaginings, or something more, I cannot say for certain. In light of later events, I would settle for the latter, but you must judge for yourself when you read my manuscript. And with the mention of that, I come back to the most difficult bit of all, Matthew's death.

I will just state the bare facts, if you don't mind. I think I can manage that.

Matthew died on March 10th, a year ago. He died on the river he loved in a kayaking accident. For some reason, I do not know, he went on the river at one of the most dangerous times of the year, against local advice. I was with the rescue craft when his kayak was discovered. It took longer for Matthew's body to be found, as it had been sucked right under the rock face, where it was wedged tightly in a crevice by the strong current.

He is buried in the commune's cemetery, just behind the secondary school where he taught, and right next to the remains of the old abbey.

I contacted his father, his mother died some years ago from breast cancer, but I got no response. He is in the last stages of dementia, and the manager of the care home was adamant that he could neither make any decisions nor travel to the funeral. The manager's letter was very terse and cold, and left me feeling quite bereft. Silly, I know. After all I had never met Matthew's father, he was nothing to me. Perhaps it was more to do with feeling cut off again from all I had once known, and being completely alone in a strange place. And yet, of course, it wasn't strange and I wasn't alone, but that is how it felt. I've realised over the past year that grief plays funny tricks on you. For example, I wanted to contact my parents but I didn't. I also felt quite desperate about my failure, through the Italian police, to contact Matthew's son, David, who as far as I knew still lived in Italy, with his maternal grandparents.

Odd as it may sound, Matthew's death in one way made me feel ashamed. It was if we had finally failed in our escape. We had put two fingers up to the world, and got what we deserved.

I know it's a cliche of grief but I also felt so angry. The strength of my feelings terrified me, and I was very afraid that I would end up hating Matthew for his careless destruction of our dream. I understand now that it was all part of the shock of loss, which we are never prepared for. What was it the Bard said? 'The readiness is all.' Well I wasn't ready then, and I'm not sure I am now. Nevertheless, something has changed, some healing has begun, and the answer would seem to lie in the parcel you are soon to receive.

A few days after the funeral, I took up my pen and started to write the story of the Saint. Her voice was in my head, faint but insistent, as if she was waiting, quietly and calmly, to make her presence felt. There were so many unanswered questions, and she was ready now to answer them. The words came, almost without thought, and I had never written anything, with such ease and certainty. Of course, I had been thinking about the story, trying to fill in the missing details, for a long time, and now it was there, in my head, complete, finished. All I had to do was write it down.

Writing as therapy, writing to cope with overwhelming grief. Was that all it was? Many people, you included, will probably think so. It certainly helped with the pain. I won't deny that. Every day when I got up, alone in the flat, I had something to do. The story was waiting for me, she was waiting for me. I never had to strain for her voice, just give body to it, and as I did so, my own story fell into place, became more bearable. I felt able to venture into her suffering, her sense of loss and pain, in a way that I couldn't do with my own. Centuries of time and change separated us, but the suffering remained constant, and comfort lay in revealing that. The physical act of writing also brought relief. I wrote in long hand, scribbling furiously in an A5 notebook, encased in the soft, black, leather cover, Matthew had bought for me years ago in a local bookshop. I loved to see the words building up on the page, as the story found its own momentum. Imagination and something else, indefinable, but always present, was pushing me on, so that when I sat back at the end of the day, and read over what I had written, I would exclaim in surprise over a turn the story had taken, or a thought I hadn't realised I had expressed.

I believed I was writing the book for Matthew, but now I am not so sure. His death certainly made the writing possible, a tribute to the man I had loved so completely, and so defiantly. His final gift to me perhaps. And there was comfort in that thought too. But as the story unfolded, it became more than that, more than homage to a lost love, more than therapy and comfort. I suppose what I am trying to say is that the story took over and led me away from my own pain, towards something wiser, and older, and full of life. Funnily enough, as I write these words, it is the river which is in my head, the river which Matthew died on, the river which keeps on flowing. And it is the sound of that river, blended with the saint's voice, which drove me to finish the story, or almost—

It's on its way to you now—rough and ready, but waiting to be understood.

We need your forgiveness.

Rosalind

Part Two

I. Maggie & David

When the second call came, she didn't answer it immediately. Despite being prepared, she was still a little nervous. Unlocking the past seemed a risky thing to do, although she had to admit to a certain curiosity about the boy, the man, she felt she knew, but had never met. She also didn't want to appear too eager, as if safety lay in calm detachment. Nevertheless, as she lifted the handset from the socket, she was trembling and the words caught in her throat.

'Maggie Pool speaking. Is that David?'

She had recognised the number, as it flashed up on the small, luminous screen, from the ansafone message.

'Yes, yes it is.' A very hesitant and equally nervous voice replied. 'I hope you don't mind me calling you like this, but you knew my father well, and I just wanted to—', the voice petered out into an awkward cough, and then silence.

'I understand,' Maggie said quickly, anxious to reassure the young man, her own nervousness disappearing completely in the face of his obvious embarrassment. 'I knew your father extremely well, and what's more,' she paused for a moment, 'I was very fond of him. It's good to hear from you.'

'Is it really?' David asked, his obvious relief making her smile.

'Yes, of course. We became close friends and—,' she hesitated slightly, ' he told me quite a lot about you—eventually—when he felt he could trust me.'

She didn't want David to think he had just been a topic of idle gossip. It hadn't been like that at all. The confidences, she and Matthew had shared, had been important to both of them, and she would like his son to know that.

'Can we meet?' David asked abruptly. 'I'm planning to go to France soon but I should like to talk to you first, if that's possible? I need to know more about my father, and I think you can help.'

Maggie's heart beat a little faster at the suppressed emotion in David's voice. He sounded just like Matthew.

'Yes, yes we can meet if that is what you want,' she heard herself saying, as she struggled to resist the pull of a past she thought she had put behind her. 'Where and when? I'm fairly free most days. Retirement, you know, that's what it's like.'

David laughed, more relaxed now she had agreed to meet.

'I always imagined you as someone who filled 'every unforgiving minute' with some rigorous, intellectual activity.'

Now it was Maggie's turn to laugh.

'Well, if you think that, you've got me all wrong. I'm afraid there are lots of days when I just drift and I make no apologies for that either,' she finished with mock fierceness, which made David laugh again.

They both felt it. The connection, slight as yet, a tenuous thread holding them together, and they were relieved.

'Where are you? I mean where are you ringing from?' Maggie asked.

'London,' David replied. 'A small hotel in Clapham.'

'Let's meet on the steps of The British Museum at 12 noon tomorrow,' Maggie said decisively. 'Would that suit you?'

'Fine, absolutely fine. I look forward to it,' David replied. 'And thank you, Mrs Pool, thank you.'

She was about to say 'Maggie, please' when the phone clicked and he was gone. She had half expected him to be difficult to get rid of, but no, his sudden briskness had reflected her own, and it surprised her.

The next morning Maggie was up early. She hadn't slept well, and she was glad when it grew light, and she felt the day had begun. Since she retired, she had got into the habit of waking at about seven, but not actually getting out of bed until some time after eight. In her teaching days, she was invariably up at six, and out of the house by seven fifteen, so that when that necessity no longer existed, she felt almost obliged to stay in bed an hour or two longer, just to prove to herself that she really was free at last.

On this particular morning, however, there was the dog to walk and a blouse, she had washed the night before, to iron, before she set off to catch the first off-peak train up to London, for a meeting which both excited and alarmed her.

All night, she had tossed and turned restlessly, as images from the past, held at bay for so long, swarmed into her head, jostling for the right to be seen and remembered. In order to bring some discipline to her thoughts, she tried to recall the exact layout of Layters School and the English Department, in particular. In her mind she trod those corridors again, but even though they had been so familiar, for so many years, some parts of the building proved impossible to visualise, as if they had simply dropped out of her memory, into some strange abyss.

The same thing happened to people's faces, those of students especially, whereas the faces of colleagues seemed a little more durable. The two faces, she both feared and longed to recreate, she put aside to begin with, concentrating instead on less well known staff and students, as if deliberately trying to test the accuracy and reliability of her memory.

The face of her second in department, Christine Lodge, appointed just two terms before Maggie herself retired, returned with such vividness, that Maggie felt the old loathing, like a bitter taste in her mouth, her heart pounding with renewed indignation and anger. Why is it that the faces of those we hate or despise are so much easier to recall than the faces of those whom we love? She wondered, as she drifted on the borderlands of sleep.

The effort to recall the faces of Matthew and Rosalind, as she had last seen them, nearly eighteen years ago, was making her sleepy, like counting sheep. The harder she concentrated, the more elusive they became. Even if she could fix one of their faces for a few moments in her head, it soon dissolved, like a fleeting backward glance, into a whirlpool of words and memories. She could hear their voices, Rosalind's low and musical, Matthew's strong but hesitant, as if it were yesterday, it was their features which failed to cohere.

She supposed old age might be the problem. The brain attempting to process too much information and just not managing it. She was only too familiar with the strangely physical sensation of things simply slipping from her mind, at unexpected moments. She could deal with that. She just had to wait, and after a decent interval they would return, as if intent on proving their independence from her.

This was different, however. The elusive faces were different, and it was nothing to do with old age or failing memory. She was sure of that. Something in her head was resisting her attempts to bring them back whole and alive. She could summon up echoes, glimpses of what had been, but not the whole picture. Something had to be avoided. She knew that, and she didn't even want to wonder what it was. Perhaps her meeting with David would change that. Whatever happened, it was bound to bring some things to the surface which she had thought well and truly buried, and she wondered if she was ready for that.

She caught a train at 9.45. It was still quite crowded but she managed to get a seat. The rush hour no longer seemed to finish neatly at 9 o'clock, but extended well into the morning. This late start also appeared to be matched by an equally early finish in the afternoon, and Maggie wondered when any work actually got done. She assumed it was what was now called flexi-working, a luxury, that as a full time teacher, she had never had the opportunity to enjoy. I suppose pupils could have staggered starts to the day, she mused, as the train gathered speed and her fellow travellers settled to their newspapers. But no, that wouldn't work. Schools would become too fragmented and lose their cohesive quality. Not that Layters Girls Grammar School had felt very cohesive during those last few weeks before she retired. But that was probably her fault. It had become easier as the years passed to blame herself for what happened, although she knew it wasn't the whole truth. Perhaps this meeting with David would help her to gain a better perspective on the situation, see it clearly from more points of view. Such a hope, she realised, was probably one of the reasons she had agreed to the meeting. David was right, there were still loose ends to be tied up, blanks to be filled in. The past might indeed be another country, where they do things differently, she reflected wryly, but sometimes you have to revisit it, whatever the risk.

The train was a fast one and would be in Marylebone before 10.30. She would have plenty of time to have a coffee and croissant at the small cafe she liked, almost opposite to the entrance to the museum, before she was due to meet David at twelve. That would be good. She sighed with satisfaction. She would have the chance to compose herself, and order her thoughts before the meeting.

The train was drawing into Marylebone station when another thought struck her, obvious and slightly comical. How on earth was she going to recognise David in the usual crowd of visitors, milling about on the museum steps? Matthew had once showed her a photograph of his son as a small boy, but she had no idea what he looked like now, a young man in his mid-twenties. How foolish they both were to imagine that they would know each other, through some strange intuition. They should at least have agreed to wear something distinctive, like spies trading secrets.

Heading towards the underground, Maggie was irritated by her own lack of foresight. It wasn't like her, she was usually better organised. If only David hadn't rung off so suddenly she might have had time to think of such practical details. The phone call had been too hurried, too emotional. Neither of them had been thinking straight.

She took the Bakerloo line and decided to get off at Oxford Circus. It was only just after 10.30 and she could do with a walk. She tended to think more clearly when she was walking, something she had noticed more and more as she got older. She had always been impressed by Dickens' passion for walking, pointing out to her students that he would think nothing of walking the thirty miles from London to Gad's Hill, his home in Higham, Kent. Now she understood. How many knotty problems of plot and character were resolved on those night walks, she wondered, the steady rhythm of his walking gradually beating the pieces into place? In her own small way, Maggie guessed she had experienced something similar on her long walks with the dog. She never ceased to be surprised how quickly and easily ideas, even snatches of conversation between characters, came to her while she was walking, and then she would have to work hard to keep them in her head until she got home and could jot something down.

Maggie loved writing, and had self-published three novels since she retired, more for the fun of seeing how they would turn out as real books you could pick off the shelf and read, than to make money or create a publishing sensation. To her surprise, they had been received with considerable interest and some excitement by friends and family, and particularly past students, who were keen to know if they featured in any of them. She had spent her working life studying other people's literary efforts, she felt it was time to have a go herself. It was a sobering experience and it taught her a lot. It was such hard work that she felt ashamed of her own, almost careless, critical dismissal of some writers. Even if they were flawed, they deserved more respect than she had sometimes given them. At the other extreme, the writers she loved and admired, grew even more in her estimation, and she returned to their works with renewed awe and delight.

The rush hour was over but the Tottenham Court Road was still very busy.

All those flexi workers hurrying to their late morning starts, she thought, as she walked as briskly as she could on the crowded pavement. Certainly everyone seemed very purposeful in their walking, and courteous towards others equally intent on reaching their destination. No groups of ambling tourists blocked her way, and she felt swept along by the energy of those around her. For a while she felt part of the working world again, and it invigorated her. There were many positives about retirement, and anyway she wouldn't be able to teach anything like a full timetable any more, but nevertheless, there were still things she missed quite acutely from her working life, if she allowed her mind to dwell on it. The intellectual challenge of stimulating bright, young, minds was one, and although the writing had helped to fill that need, she missed the interaction of ideas which teaching had brought her. Writing was a solitary occupation and lacked the excitement of good, old fashioned, academic argument. Over many years, in her A-Level classes, she had come into contact with quite a number of minds, so much brighter than her own, and she had loved it. She had never felt intimidated by such a situation, just grateful for the chance to stretch her own mind alongside those of her students.

It was that passion for their subject which had initially brought Maggie and Matthew together. A friendship, born out of intellectual compatibility, which became very close as time passed. Maggie had always got on well with all members of her department until Christine arrived, but with Matthew it was something more. They not only shared a love of English Literature, but also held similar views about the purpose of education. They both believed strongly in the importance of encouraging independent thought among their students, a point in which they came in direct conflict with Christine Lodge, the second in department, who had proved such a destructive presence during those last, fraught, weeks before Maggie retired. Matthew had been such a promising teacher, full of enthusiasm and ideals, and she grieved at the way his career had been cut short. It was his own fault, of course, his and Rosalind's, but that didn't prevent the sense of waste, of opportunities thrown away. In the immediate aftermath of his elopement with Rosalind, and earlier still, of course, on the Haworth trip, she had felt such a confusion of emotion, that she found it impossible to make any clear judgement on what had happened, and more importantly, what she had felt about it. She was angry, of course, at her own folly, as well as his, and still deeply upset, although not shocked, by the lovemaking she had witnessed. For days, weeks, even longer, it didn't take much for her to recall all the details of that day, with a vividness, which hurt her heart, and left her tearful and distracted. The walk to a ruined farmhouse, the supposed site of Wuthering Heights, was meant to be a relaxing culmination to the year 12 Bronte trip, organised by herself and Matthew. It turned out to be the crisis point in her long, and generally successful teaching career.

Barely aware of other pedestrians, as they pursued their own inner lives alongside her, she saw again the two, moving bodies, faintly luminous in the gloom, and felt again the jolt of recognition, which accompanied a long- held fear. She realised now that she had always known Matthew and Rosalind were lovers. She had just refused to acknowledge it. Coming upon them like that had been more of a humiliation than a shock, and even at a distance of seventeen years, her cheeks grew hot at the thought of that day. She hated to be regarded as a prurient voyeur, but in the end she was only doing her professional duty. Rosalind was in her care and it should never have happened. Of course, Matthew was to blame too, more than anyone, a fact that Maggie had been determined to make clear when she went to visit him in his room that evening.

Quickening her pace, to still the agitation in her head, or was it her heart, she became aware that she had already passed Tottenham Court Road underground station and would soon need to turn left into Bloomsbury Street. She was only minutes away from The British Museum, where, at 12 o'clock, David,

Matthew's son, would be waiting for her. After the elopement, Matthew and what he had meant to her, had been put away somewhere where she couldn't touch it. She had wanted to sometimes, particularly after Tom's death, but she had stood firm. If she needed comfort in the bleak hours of widowhood, she had no right to look for it there. But now Matthew was dead, and his son wanted to see her.

Like that moment, high on the Yorkshire moor, when she was drawn inexorably towards a discovery she didn't want to make, she felt once again the apprehension and the fear, but had no power to resist. Matthew and Rosalind had treated her badly, but strangely perhaps, she still felt she owed them something. All those years ago, she had been the one in charge, the mature, experienced, older colleague, who had let everyone down, including herself. Now, perhaps, with David there was a chance to put something right. She wasn't clear what, but she had to try.

Turning right off Bloomsbury Road, towards the museum, she made her way to the small, Italian cafe she liked. It had taken her just over twenty minutes to walk from Oxford Circus and she still had another hour to fill.

Despite her anxiety, in the end it was all so easy. No need for flowers in buttonholes, or brightly coloured items of clothing because Maggie recognised him immediately. She had got to the museum steps at five minutes to twelve. They weren't so crowded as usual, but as she arrived so did a large party of Chinese students, and for a few moments she found herself caught up in their excited volubility, as they were swept towards the entrance, the leader of their party waving them forward in a peremptory manner. Extricating herself from the tail end of the group, she saw him. He was entering the gates of the museum, and looking anxiously towards the steps, as if fearing he was late.

The likeness was startling. She had expected some similarity in appearance, but not this. The young man, fast approaching her, walked with Matthew's stride, his head down, and his shoulders slightly hunched. He was dressed casually but not shabbily. Just like his father, she thought, who had, as far as she could remember, never worn a tie for teaching, but always looked neat and tidy, nevertheless. The only thing which was unruly was his thick, dark, hair, through which he would run his fingers repeatedly, whenever he was nervous or angry. His son had the same dark hair, but his was combed back neatly from his forehead and showed no sign of being ruffled by anything. Matthew, as a young man, was so obviously present in David, that Maggie assumed he would recognise her just as easily. For a few moments she forgot completely that they had no personal history in common beyond Matthew, and smiling at him, she waited for the expected greeting. Instead he walked straight past, gently brushing against her shoulder in his hurry, as he leapt lightly up the steps.

'David, I'm here,' she called after him. 'It's me Maggie, Maggie Pool.'

It was awkward, the conversation between them, to begin with. They both started apologising, barely registering what the other was saying. Words seemed the only defence against a shy embarrassment, which gripped them both as they hovered rather foolishly on the top step, outside the museum. People moved and talked around them, some rushing impatiently past them, as if they were in the way, but they remained isolated in their own small world, uncertain of what to do next.

Maggie broke the spell.

'I've just had coffee, but if you would like something, we

could try one of the places in the museum. Hopefully they won't be too crowded.'

'No, I'm fine. Let's walk instead,' David said more firmly than she had expected. 'It might be easier to talk if we do.'

Maggie cast a quick, sidelong, look at the young man, surprised by his sensitivity to the obvious awkwardness of the situation. And yet that was like his father too, especially when there had been tensions in the department and Maggie needed his support.

'Good idea,' she replied. 'There are some quiet squares in Bloomsbury, where we can wander. We might even find a seat to sit on if we're lucky.'

He was right. It was easier to talk when they were walking, despite the noise of traffic and the continual need to dodge pedestrians. It was a bit like talking in a car. There was no need to face each other and that made difficult moments more manageable. And there were some, as Maggie had feared there would be.

It was apparent very quickly that David was angry, not with her particularly, but with life in general. As soon as they started walking, he began to talk. To begin with, he didn't seem to want any comment from Maggie, and for a time she was content just to listen. The time would come when she would have to speak, put things straight, but that could wait. It was obvious that for David there were things he had to say and she was the audience he had chosen.

In a way, she felt flattered, even touched, just as she had by Matthew's respect and affection, which had quickly become such an important part of their relationship. Time is so fluid, she thought, as she matched her stride to that of the young man beside her. Her meeting with David had brought the past flooding back; its events, its crises, and above all its emotions.

Scenes she had put aside for so long, returned in all their original vividness, and she felt her heart quicken with unresolved pain and desire.

David's anger seemed mostly directed against his parents, which wasn't surprising, Maggie thought, as in a sense they had both abandoned him. She knew that Matthew hadn't seen his son since he was a toddler, although he had certainly kept some sort of contact until the boy was eight. She knew no more after that, as it was then Matthew disappeared completely from her life, and with him all news of his son. She had always thought it conceivable that he maintained the contact while in France with Rosalind, but she had no way of knowing if that was actually so. Now, listening to David, she realised that contact had indeed been dropped all those years ago, and much of David's sadness and anger sprang from that fact. It was clear that David felt that his father had never really loved him. If he had, how could he have abandoned him in that way?

Despite David's obvious reluctance to be interrupted, Maggie felt she had to speak. She knew, without a doubt, that Matthew had loved his son, and David must know it too. That was one part of the picture she could put right.

In their walking, they had taken little heed of where they were going, but when they reached a quiet square, with a small, enclosed garden, open to the public and containing a wooden bench, conveniently out of sight of passers by, she immediately steered Matthew towards such a welcome refuge.

She turned to look at the face, so new to her and yet so familiar.

'Your father loved you. While I knew him, he never stopped loving you, and even when he disappeared from my sight, I have every reason to believe he continued to do so. If you believe anything, you must believe that. I knew him very well and you are so like him.'

David coloured at Maggie's words and hung his head, in the sheepish manner, so characteristic of his father.

'Why then did he not come to see me? I know he ended up in France, my grandparents told me. Surely it's not that difficult to travel from France to Italy?' he finished bitterly, raising his eyes to meet Maggie's.

'I'm sure he had his reasons,' she said hesitantly, 'but I'm not the one who can give them to you, Rosalind is.'

'Is she the slut he went off with?' David asked viciously, his voice charged with hatred.

Maggie was shocked. David had appeared such a mild mannered, shy, young man, despite all his suppressed anger and inability to stop talking. She guessed the violence of the outburst was uncharacteristic, but it certainly showed how deep the hurt was. David looked unrepentant, but was obviously uncomfortable with his behaviour, and wary of Maggie's reaction.

For a few minutes, the silence hung heavily between them. Maggie knew she had to think carefully before she spoke, if she was to be fair to everyone. How she described the relationship between Matthew and Rosalind could have a lasting effect on how David felt about his father, and she didn't want to get it wrong.

'The girl's name was Rosalind,' she said at last. 'How much do you know about her?'

'Nothing really,' David muttered.' I don't think my father wanted me to know anything. I hope he was too ashamed.'

Maggie, trying to keep calm, ignored David's last remark. Instead she began to talk quietly about Rosalind as a student. How interesting and able she was, her passion for the Brontes, her respect and admiration for Matthew as a teacher, her willingness to take responsibility for the affair which took over their lives.

'In no way was Rosalind a slut. She was a fine young woman,' Maggie added firmly and proudly. 'You must not think of her like that.'

'Why not?' David replied. ' she seduced my father and wrecked his career.'

That's not true or fair,' Maggie said hastily. 'They fell in love. They were both romantics. It shouldn't have happened but it did. I think they felt they had no choice but to run away.'

There's always a choice,' David replied, more tearful than angry now. 'If he hadn't run away with that girl—Rosalind—he might have had more time for me. I never knew my father and now he's gone. How am I supposed to feel? Can you tell me that?'

'No, I can't', said Maggie sadly, laying a hand on David's arm. 'But I can tell you what I know about your father and Rosalind, and what happened between them. Things are always different from how they appear, and I would like you to get as near the truth as you can. Perhaps then, you will begin to understand.'

David stood up and walked restlessly to and fro in front of Maggie.

'You want to defend my father—and that woman, don't you? I can't see why when they obviously betrayed you too. It doesn't make sense.'

Maggie's neck muscles tensed and she felt a niggling pain above her right eye. Here it comes, she thought. The moment I have put off for over seventeen years. And there was no way of stopping it, she knew that, and in a funny sort of way, it was quite a relief.

'Yes, it does make sense,' Maggie said abruptly, turning away from David who had come to a halt in front of her, and focusing instead on the black, metal bin, overflowing with rubbish, which should have been collected days before.

'I loved them. I had every reason to want to defend them. I felt very close to both of them, in different ways. Your father was a colleague, no, a friend, with whom I quickly developed a special, professional, bond. We thought alike about so many things, kindred spirits, in the true sense of the word. I grew to rely on him, perhaps too much, particularly after Christine arrived. She was appointed as my second in department, and from the moment I first set eyes on her, I knew we wouldn't get on. Unlike your father, she had no genuine love of literature, no desire to inspire her students with passion and delight for the texts they were studying. In fact I don't think she really liked students or teaching. Basically, she was just an administrator and her philistine ways drew your father and I even closer together. She recognised the bond we had, and it made her both jealous and vindictive, but more of that when I get to Haworth.'

Maggie paused for a moment. She realised that she was talking much more quickly than usual, and that Matthew was also listening very intently. He had sat down on the bench beside her again when she came to a halt, and urged her to continue.

'Tell it all,' he said, rather hoarsely. 'Don't leave anything out.'

She nodded, afraid to go on, but compelled to do so.

'With Rosalind it was quite different. There was necessarily a professional distance between us, and we both respected that. I was a teacher and she was an exceptional student, and that was a relationship I had experienced many times before in my career. I knew how to handle it, and there was no confusion, as there was with your father over where professional warmth ended and personal intimacy began. I knew Rosalind was a particularly talented student of literature, and I wanted to nurture that talent. She had spirit and imagination, and could think in such an original way about the books she was studying. She got particularly caught up in the story of Charlotte Bronte's infatuation with Monsieur Heger, an ill-fated affair, if ever there was one. Rosalind seemed able to identify completely with Charlotte's experience, to an extent that I had never seen before. Of course, I realised later that it was her own passion for your father which gave her this insight. I believe she saw a clear parallel between her experience and that of the much revered author, and that her wish to emulate her heroine, increased the intensity of her love for your father. She was a true romantic after all.'

Circling the difficult truth, Maggie tried deliberately to lighten the tone a little.

'Anyway, a trip to Haworth was planned for year 12, as they were all studying the Brontes. I was in charge but your father did most of the work before we went. By that time I already had my suspicions about your father and Rosalind, but no hard proof. It was the trip to Haworth which was to give me that.'

Maggie paused again, embarrassed by the tremble in her voice and uncertain how to go on.

'Just say it. Don't worry about me,' David said, in little more than a whisper.

'If you can say it, I can hear it.'

'Then I'm not sure I can, but I'll try,' Maggie replied, glancing quickly at David. He was very pale, biting his lower lip repeatedly, until tiny beads of blood appeared.

'Looking back now, I think the Haworth trip was a mistake,' Maggie said slowly. She was beginning to pick her words more carefully and she sensed David was aware of that. 'We had a party of impressionable young women, whom we actively encouraged to immerse themselves in the emotional maelstrom of those Bronte lives. Fortunately, most of them were able to deal with it, but not Rosalind. I was particularly concerned about her when we visited the church at Haworth. She seemed so upset by the early deaths of the Bronte children, as if she had become fully aware of her own mortality for the first time. Some sort of emotional crisis seemed almost inevitable after that.'

Maggie sighed. Perhaps what happened later was no more than a flight from death after all. It would be a relief to leave it at that, but she knew that she couldn't. David was waiting. She had to go on.

'On the last day of our visit to Haworth,' Maggie continued, 'we had planned a walk to Top Withens, the supposed site of Emily Bronte's Wuthering Heights.

I must admit I had some misgivings about it, as the girls had tended to become too intense about the whole Bronte phenomenon, and I had been doing my best to calm things down. I asked your father, and Hannah, another young teacher, who had come with us on the trip, what they thought, and they were all for it. I think they just felt it was a good way for the girls to become acquainted with the countryside, which had helped shape the Bronte girls' imaginations, particularly Emily's. So I gave in, but I felt uneasy.'

'You had a sort of premonition? Is that it?' David said, also trying hard to relieve the tension building between them.

'Perhaps,' Maggie said carefully. 'You can call it that if you like. I just don't know. It was an odd feeling, that's all. The weather didn't help either. It was reasonable when we set off the next day, but steadily deteriorated as it approached noon. We had hoped for a leisurely lunch at Top Withens, soaking up the atmosphere, but with the wind picking up and the sky darkening, it was decided to head back to Haworth as quickly as possible. It was then that your father and Rosalind disappeared off the radar, so to speak, and I went back to look for them. I didn't want to go, but I had to. I think I knew what I was going to find. And I did. In a dark corner, in those desolate ruins, I found them going at it, like farmyard beasts in their stall. The fools, the stupid, unthinking fools. Your father saw me standing there and I can't begin to describe the look which passed between us. It shook me to the core. All I wanted to do was to escape, and erase the whole scene from my mind. I couldn't, of course. There were too many consequences--------- terrible consequences------'.

Maggie stopped. She couldn't say any more. Tears, held back for nearly two decades, ran freely down her cheeks, and she buried her face in her hands, sobbing like a child.

It was a long time before either of them could speak. David, embarrassed and upset, by Maggie's sudden collapse, wanted to comfort her. Hesitantly, he put his arm round her shoulders, feeling how bony she was, through her light raincoat.

With the awkwardness of youth, he hoped no-one would see them. His own turmoil of feeling, he couldn't confront yet. He simply wanted the tears to stop.

'It's all right, everything's all right,' he said at last. 'You've told me now. It's over. There is no need to cry.'

'But there's more,' Maggie replied, almost angrily, wiping her flushed cheeks with her sodden handkerchief. 'That's not it. If only it were.'

'More, what do you mean more?' David said, removing his arm from Maggie's shoulders and moving back a little on the bench.

'I had no right to use those words about your father and Rosalind. After all, I'm no better. That's what I mean.'

David stared at Maggie, terrified of yet another revelation, and knowing instinctively that it was going to be much, much, worse.

'That evening,' Maggie was whispering now. 'I went to see your father in his room. I needed to confront him with what I had witnessed at Top Withens, make him realise that he had to finish his relationship with Rosalind at once, or I would be unable to save him. I suspected that Christine, my second in department, had already guessed that something was going on, and I knew she would stop at nothing to ruin me if she could. Your father had played right into her hands.'

David leaned forward a little, anxious to catch every word, his back aching with the tension.

'You wanted to save him. Why? Why would you do that? Risk your professional position for a man who had been so foolish?' David's puzzlement was almost comical in its naivety.

'Because I loved him. I loved him. Surely you realise that?'

'So what happened? What did you do? Tell me. Tell me. I have to know.'

David had grabbed Maggie's shoulders, and was shaking her, gently but firmly, as if to dislodge the words by force.

'We made love. Your father and I made love. For that one night only we were lovers.'

David said nothing, as his world shifted again, and Maggie wept.

II. MARIA & STEPHEN

It all started with Stephen's age. That was the catalyst, a trivial piece of information, tossed out carelessly, as a bit of social chit chat. Stephen was nineteen, the same age as Matthew when she married him. No one noticed the number but Maria, during the slightly nervous, but hearty introductions Jeannie Gale made, as soon as they arrived. It was a lunch party, because of David, and they had been asked for 12.30. Maria was already feeling tense and fearful from the heat, and as Stephen stepped forward to shake hands, his aunt's words fell like a hot brand on an already smouldering fire.

'This is my nephew, Stephen. He's spending the summer with us, after a year out, and before going up to Oxford. He will be nineteen in just over a week's time, so we can have a double celebration.'

She smiled at Maria, as Stephen, looking a little awkward, held out his hand. For a moment, it seemed as if she wouldn't take it, but then she too smiled as their fingers touched, in the lightest of greetings.

'You're the swimmer, I believe. I've seen you sometimes from the bottom of our garden.'

The young man looked startled, going a deep red under his tan.

'I didn't realise we were so easily overlooked,' he said, almost apologetically, as if it was somehow his fault that he had intruded on her notice.

'I wasn't spying. Don't think that,' Maria continued hastily. 'It was the swimming. I just enjoyed watching the swimming.'

'Well, we can all swim this afternoon, if you like,' Jeannie interrupted gaily, a little disconcerted by the conversation, and a strange tension between the young people.

'I don't swim,' Maria said abruptly, 'not any more. The sun, it's the sun, it gets too hot'.

'I understand,' Stephen replied swiftly. 'There's no need to. You can sit in the shade and watch. Does your son like the water? After all it is meant to be his birthday party.'

'Yes, yes he does.'

The kindness in his voice made her feel tearful and angry at the same time, and she turned away to look for David, who had already slipped out through the open door onto the terrace, and was teetering on the edge of the pool.

Following her gaze, and seeing the look of panic in her eyes, Stephen was out of the door before she had time to move. She watched as he approached the boy calmly and taking his hand, led him towards the shallow end, where broad, semi-circular, steps led down gently into the pool. David was obviously asking to have a swim because Stephen had bent down and was unbuckling the child's sandals and pulling his T shirt over his head. Maria made no attempt to intervene, although she had followed Stephen out of the door, and was standing in the narrow band of shade cast by the house. She knew, without thinking, that David was safe in Stephen's hands, and with that realisation came a pain of recognition, which swept her back seven years to a cold, damp, city, and to another young man who was almost nineteen, and who had captured her with his kindness.

Maria's skin was burning hot, and as she felt the touch of cool brickwork through her thin, cotton blouse, she shivered violently. A wave of nausea passed over her, and she put a hand on the wall to steady herself. The blue glare of the swimming pool hurt her eyes, and she fumbled in her skirt pocket for her sunglasses. It was all coming back, those terrible months before David was born, and she knew she couldn't bear it. The throb in her head kept time with the pulsing waves of light which raced towards her, pinning her against the wall, until she felt she would suffocate with the pressure.

David was in the water now, splashing happily on the shallow steps. She could see that he was shouting, the black hole of his mouth, opening and closing like a stranded fish, but no words reached her. A stifling blanket of silence had enveloped her, and she struggled to call out to him.

Stephen, too, was now undressing, stepping out of his trousers and unbuttoning his shirt, as he waved excitedly to the boy in the pool. All his movements were a strange blend of diffidence and enthusiasm, and as Maria watched him scoop up the laughing child, and push forward into deeper water, a familiar sense of loss left her breathless.

Lunch was delayed because of David and Stephen's swim. No one seemed to mind. It was so hot, and as Jeannie said laughing, the food was all cold. It didn't really matter when they had it, they could just pick at something when they felt hungry. It was meant to be a picnic after all, and picnics were usually quite movable feasts. The Gales and Maria's parents had remained indoors, enjoying a sparkling white wine, Richard Gale wanted them to try. The conversation which had been a little forced at first, was now more comfortable, particularly between the two women.

'I'm just so sorry we haven't got together before', Jeannie had said when Sally and Bernardo first arrived. 'I hope we can make up for it now'.

From that moment on she had made every effort to make her guests feel at home, and pleasant as such attention was, Sally wondered what really lay behind Jeannie's warmth and hospitality. She didn't have to wait long for an answer.

'I'm really keen for Stephen to get to know your daughter,' she confessed, when the young people had disappeared, and the four of them were comfortably settled in the living room. 'He has been staying with us for some weeks now but hasn't really made any friends locally. It's quite difficult, I suppose, when we are all cut off in our own little ivory towers. He's reading a lot, of course, ready for Oxford and he swims. He's in a county team at home, I believe, so it's some sort of training schedule. But it's not enough for a young man, he should be with other young people a bit more. Don't you agree?'

She looked anxiously at Sally, as if she couldn't continue without her approval. 'Well, yes, I do,' Sally replied hesitantly. She knew she was approaching dangerous ground, and would have to pick her way carefully. Despite the frequent tension between herself and Maria, Sally was very protective of her daughter, and reluctant to expose her vulnerability to more people than necessary.

'Of course, Maria is a bit older than Stephen,' she said after a moment or two, 'and she has David. She also finds social situations, meeting new people, a bit difficult sometimes.'

She had spoken a little more freely than she intended, but Jeannie's own need for reassurance seemed to suggest that she would be sympathetic towards Maria's problems.

'I see,' Jeannie said quietly. 'Is this something you're happy to talk about? I don't want to pry.'

'You're not,' Sally said quite briskly, 'but it's perhaps best left for another day. Things seem to be all right at the moment.'

She looked towards the open doors and the swimming pool as she spoke, where the heads of Stephen and David, bobbed like corks, on top of the water, and David's shrieks of delight added weight to her words. There was no sign of Maria but she guessed she had sought the shade somewhere, and was watching her son, from some point, out of sight.

'Your nephew certainly has a way with children,' she said, smiling at Jeannie. 'Perhaps we can hire him for a few hours each day. I don't think I've seen David so happy for a long time.'

'I'm glad, 'Jeannie replied.' It is his birthday after all, it needs to be special. We are so pleased you were willing to share it with us.'

'It's good for us too,' Sally replied generously. 'We don't socialise a lot at the moment, it's not easy with a young child, and Maria is a little reluctant to be left on her own with him.'

'I understand,' Jeannie replied, although she didn't really. What could be so difficult about a mother staying alone at home with her child occasionally, while her parents went out? The whole situation seemed a little odd, and she wondered if she had been very wise in trying to get Stephen and Maria together. If the girl had problems, and he started to get involved, things might get difficult. Jeannie was fond of her nephew, but she didn't really know him all that well.

She was also rather intimidated by his intellect, although she would never have admitted it to anyone. He was planning to read English Literature at Oxford, and Jeannie, not being a great reader herself, found it almost impossible to chat to him about the books he was reading. Her own knowledge of English Literature had ended at GCSE, and on the one occasion when she had taken a furtive look at the titles of some of the books, piled on his bedside table, she hadn't recognised any of them. He was her sister Clare's son, and it had been quite a rash gesture when she had offered to have him for the summer. She was sure both Stephen and his mother would turn down the offer, and she was surprised when they both appeared to jump at the chance.

'It will be such a good opportunity for him to do some quiet study, before he begins his course,' Clare said, sounding really grateful for once. The two sisters didn't always get on very well, as Clare had been highly critical, on occasions, of her younger sister's self- indulgent lifestyle. Jeannie and Richard, who had taken early retirement from the civil service, had no children of their own, and were consequently pretty well off. Richard had been diagnosed with a heart condition, a leaky aortic valve, nearly four years ago, and after surgery, they had sold their house in Guildford, and put the money towards a villa in Italy, and a leisurely retirement in the sun.

Jeannie had always felt that her sister put too much pressure on Stephen, her only son, to succeed academically, and it was largely because of her instinctive sympathy for her nephew's situation, as the object of such intense, parental, pressure, that she had decided to invite Stephen to spend the summer with them. When her offer was accepted, she was full of misgivings, but on the whole, things hadn't turned out too badly. Stephen seemed happy to study and swim and the lack of any social life didn't seem to bother him. It was only Jeannie who was concerned about that, and now she had done something about it, and so far the day seemed to be a success.

* * *

Outside, Maria was still struggling. She had ventured out of the shade, in an attempt to break through the wall of silence cutting her off from the scene being played out in front of her. It was if David and Stephen were in some sort of parallel world she couldn't quite reach, and although she knew they were both calling to her, she couldn't respond.

Moving to the side of the pool, she knelt down on the hot stones, and splashed her face with the cold water. Nobody bothered to heat their pools, but instead they relied on the constant sun. As she looked up, a sudden attack of giddiness made her sway drunkenly on the edge of the pool, until a steadying hand grasped her arm and pushed her back, as water from Stephen's quick movement splashed the front of her blouse and trickled down between her breasts. With this contact came the return of sound, and Maria felt the tight band, which was squeezing the breath out of her, loosen and drop away.

'I'm sorry, I didn't mean to splash you but I thought you were about to join us in the water, and I'm not sure that's what you intended.'

The concern in Stephen's eyes was lightened by the humour in his words, as he hung onto the side of the pool next to her.

'No. I was just trying to cool down. It's so hot.'

Her voice seemed to come from a great distance, and she wondered if he could hear her. While she was speaking, he had turned away and was watching David who was back on the curved steps. The boy was jumping excitedly from one step to another, his small body almost obscured by his splashing.

'Be careful,' Stephen shouted, making Maria's heart jump with panic, 'or you will slip. Time to get out now.'

He pushed off from the side of the pool, looking up at Maria, as he did so.

'I'd better see to him. Are you okay now?'

'Yes, yes of course. Thanks.'

She watched as Stephen fetched a towel from a nearby chair to wrap the boy in. Although it was a hot day she could see that David was shivering. He had been too long in the cold water.

Getting to her feet, another wave of giddiness hit Maria, something in her mind slipped, and the years rolled back. Within seconds, she was at her son's side, where to Stephen's shocked surprise, she pushed the boy away so roughly that he tripped on the end of the towel, and fell heavily on to the stone tiles, hitting his head with a sickening thud.

Maria barely gave her son a glance as she threw herself at Stephen, beating on his wet chest with her fists.

'Now look what you've left me with—a child. You never said there would be a child. It's not what we agreed. You bastard! You bastard! You lying, cheating bastard!'

Her voice, distorted by anger and grief was hardly more than a croak, but amplified by the walls surrounding the pool, it became a cry of torment.

Fending off Maria's blows with one hand, as best he could, Stephen turned to look at David. The boy was sitting up, deathly pale, his eyes wide with horror at what his mother was doing. A trickle of blood trailed down his neck from a cut on the back of his head, and his violent shivering was now more the result of fear, than cold.

'Mamma, stop! Stop! Please stop!'

Some note of terror in his high pitched voice seemed to bring Maria back a little from her own nightmare. Her arms dropped to her sides, and she began to cry, her chest heaving with harsh, dry, sobs.

For a few minutes Stephen felt locked in a scene he couldn't escape. The terrified child and the sobbing woman had become part of a triangle of pain, which he had been forced to join as some sort of substitute or stand-in. For the moment he would have to play the part, he had no other choice.

Putting out a hand, he helped David to his feet, wrapping the trampled towel around his shaking body. As he did so, he was aware of someone else at his side, and with a sense of relief, he realised that Sally was gently removing the boy from his embrace, and leading him towards the villa. Jeannie had also appeared, but seemed uncertain about how to approach Maria, whose clenched fists and loud sobbing, signalled defiance and resistance, rather than a need for comfort. While Jeannie hesitated, Stephen moved forward and enclosed Maria in his arms. Every muscle in her body tensed itself against him, as she struggled to escape, but he hung on, grimly and instinctively. It wasn't over yet. He guessed the real crisis was still to come.

To begin with, Bernardo and Richard had left it to the women, but when it became obvious that Jeannie didn't know how to handle the situation, Bernardo knew he would have to act. He had always found his only daughter difficult, despite loving her with all the passion of an Italian father, but since her illness their relationship had broken down completely. He found her sudden changes of mood unsettling and impossible to predict, and he resented the way she had kept Sally and himself trapped in the villa, deprived of all social engagements, from the fear she wouldn't cope. His surprise was therefore considerable when both his wife and daughter agreed to accept the Gales' invitation, and although he was pleased by this return to some kind of normality, he had still viewed the venture with a certain degree of trepidation. Now his worst fears had been confirmed, and he was obliged to step in and rescue the situation. It wasn't fair to leave it to Stephen. Bernardo liked the young man, but he had only just met Maria, and he could hardly be expected to deal with one of her 'turns', let alone understand her.

Bernardo knew that his daughter was damaged, and that he shared some responsibility for that. The rest of the blame lay with the young man, who had got her pregnant, while he was still a penniless student. Angry with both his daughter and her lover, Matthew, he had insisted that they marry before the child was born, but it had been a mistake. The marriage seemed to mark the end of something, not the beginning. He had also insisted that Maria abandon her course in Politics and Economics and leave Durham immediately. That was wrong too; he knew that now. At the time, all he could think of was securing respectability for his daughter, and then separating her from the man who had jeopardised it. Looking back, his actions appeared old fashioned and draconian, and he knew they were partly responsible for destroying the feelings, which had brought Maria and Matthew together in the first place.

It was hard to say when the first signs of mental instability became apparent. After David was born, Maria had suffered badly from post-natal depression, refusing to see Matthew, and becoming very detached from David, a detachment which occasionally became quite hostile. Sally and Bernardo realised that Maria was never going to be able to look after David on her own, as sometimes her indifference to her son's presence was quite frightening, and would certainly put the child at risk. So when David was two, Bernardo had persuaded Sally that it was time for them to make their permanent home in Italy, taking Maria and David with them. He had felt guilty about severing the final links between father and child, but there seemed no other alternative. The relationship between Maria and Matthew had totally disintegrated, and any mention of her estranged husband now sent Maria into violent, hysterical, outbursts, which upset all of them, particularly David.

Once in Italy, Bernardo had hoped that his daughter would

recover with quiet and rest in a warm climate, but the opposite happened. Maria gradually began to develop a strange phobia about heat and light, as if all her fears and anxieties, were generated by the sun, and she could only find peace in the cool and dark. They thought of moving, but it wasn't practical, and her doctor advised against it.

'If it isn't heat and light which is the focus for her paranoia, it will be something else', he said one morning when Maria had been particularly reluctant to leave her room. 'If you move, you will simply take the problem with you. I think you would do better to manage it here. With time, and the right medication things may improve. If not, we may need to resort to more drastic remedies.'

Bernardo, nervous in the face of all things medical, didn't like to ask what such drastic remedies would entail. He was sure he would find the answer unbearable. For the moment they could manage, as Sally had none of his fear of illness, and handled her daughter with a gentle firmness, which kept things stable most of the time. She was also good with David, who deprived of a natural closeness with both of his parents, clung to his grandmother with a devotion which was heartbreaking.

Now, faced with his daughter, sobbing uncontrollably in another man's arms, Bernardo was greatly relieved that his wife had removed David, so swiftly and calmly, from the scene. The child had suffered enough, and he mustn't witness whatever might come next.

'Shall we get her inside?' Bernardo said quietly to Stephen, over Maria's head, which was now pressed against Stephen's chest, as she grew tired of trying to escape from his firm embrace.

'Yes, of course,' Stephen replied, feeling slightly awkward talking about Maria in the third person, as if she had no will of her own.

In the meantime, Jeannie and Richard had returned indoors and were hovering anxiously by the doors into the dining room, where an elaborate buffet was laid out on an oval table. In the middle of the feast, a magnificent cake, in the shape of a car, and adorned with six candles, was raised up on a pedestal plate, above the rest of the food.

On the phone to Sally, Jeannie had spoken of modest refreshments, and a cake for David. Now, looking at the table, a riot of colour, and laden with dishes designed to appeal to every sense, she wondered if she had gone too far. Sally and Bernardo would probably think she was showing off and she hadn't meant to. She had wanted to make a good impression but that was different. They were new acquaintances, hopefully soon to be friends, and it was important to make a reasonable effort. Now it looked as if the whole occasion was about to be ruined. Maria was obviously unwell, the child hurt, and everyone's nerves jangled. Nobody was going to feel like lunch.

In her frustration, she pulled the door to the dining room closed behind her and Richard, as Maria came into the living room, escorted by the two men. Head bowed and sobbing quietly, Maria sank, exhausted, into the first chair she came to. Stephen fetched a glass of water from the sideboard, and Bernardo sat down next to his daughter, holding her hand. No one spoke, as a strange calm descended on the scene.

It was David who shattered it. He was still very pale and had a large bump on the back of his head, but no other signs of concussion, as far as Sally could see. She knew she would have to keep a very close eye on him for the next twenty four hours, and call the doctor immediately if he vomited or appeared unnaturally sleepy. All the time she was bathing his head, and helping him to dress, he seemed anxious to return to the others, particularly Stephen. Sally, afraid of what might be happening with Maria, wanted to keep the boy away from anymore upsetting scenes, but eventually his agitation became so marked she had to give in.

They entered the living room from the patio, David immediately running towards Stephen, who had returned to the sideboard to pour himself a drink.

'My cake. Is it time for my cake?' David cried, hurling himself so hard against Stephen's legs, that the young man staggered back against the sideboard, spilling his drink, and knocking over a newly opened, bottle of red wine.

Everyone seemed to move at once, shocked out of their stillness by the boy's sudden appearance. Wine dripped from the top of the sideboard, and Jeannie went to fetch a cloth to mop up the red pool, slowly expanding across the pale, tiled, floor. Stephen grabbed David's hand and pulled him away, afraid that the child would only add to the mess. David was surprisingly resistant, staring at the encroaching tide of red, with childish horror.

' Is it blood Stephen? Is it blood?'

Bernardo and Richard were also both on their feet, as was Sally, who had followed David into the living room. Everyone looked at the boy, as he gazed in fascination at the spilt wine. It was then that the screaming began. It started as a low keening, like some wounded animal crying in the dark, but as it grew louder, the agony became unmistakably human. David shrank back against Stephen, terrified, his own screams joining his mother's, as he pointed first at the wine, and then at Maria.

III. Matthew & Rosalind

The day Matthew showed her the cave didn't start well. She had stayed up until three the night before, writing, and she woke with a headache. The late September sun, filtered through the half opened blinds, lay in bands of light across the duvet, and as she shifted a little in the bed, they danced maliciously before her eyes, like the onset of a migraine. From the kitchen she could hear the rattle of cups, and the bang of a cupboard door. Matthew was making the coffee, so it must be Saturday. Why couldn't he move about more quietly, she thought, with growing irritation. When she got up first, she always tried to creep around without a sound, closing doors and drawers with such care, that her muscles became tense with the strain. Matthew, however, seemed determined to wake her and let her know he was already up and busy. It was all right for him, he had gone to bed several hours before her. No wonder he felt refreshed. She knew she was being unreasonable, but that insight didn't prevent her from snapping at him, as soon as he entered the room, steaming mugs of coffee in his hands and a grin on his face.

'You could have let me sleep a little longer, instead of

banging around in the kitchen like some rampaging elephant,' she said fretfully, as he put her mug down on the bedside table and went to pull up the blinds. 'And don't let all that sun in, it's hurting my eyes,' she continued, reaching for her glasses and knocking the mug of coffee as she did so. 'Now look what you've made me do. It's gone all over my book.'

Fretfulness had turned into a kind of childish tearfulness, as Rosalind removed the dripping book, and dabbed rather ineffectually at the brown pool, which had begun to disappear over the edge of the table in a steady drip.

'Leave it,' Matthew said sternly. 'I'll get a cloth. What on earth's got into you this morning?'

He didn't wait for a reply, and she heard more cupboard doors bang as he searched for a cloth.

What had got into her? Matthew was quite right, she was being totally unreasonable. After all it was the start of the weekend, she was with the man she loved, the sun was shining. What could possibly be wrong? Perhaps it was just tiredness, plus a certain amount of frustration. She had worked late the previous evening because the writing wasn't going well. The words wouldn't say what she wanted them to, and she wasn't sure whether it was because she had simply run out of ideas, or the characters themselves were going on strike. It had happened before, when she was experimenting with some short stories, and she had just abandoned them. She felt reluctant to do the same with her present work. It would be too dispiriting. She was trying to write her first novel, something she felt she had put off for too long. She had the main idea, she had the outline of a story, she had some characters; it should all work. She had written the first few chapters very quickly, surprised by her own fluency and imaginative energy, but then she had come to a stop. She still had the story very clearly in her head, but the characters simply didn't want to go along with it. At the same time, ideas for alternative storylines had totally deserted her, as if they too were in revolt. Writer's block, they call it. It felt more like desertion, or even betrayal.

Refusing to give up, she had sat for several hours at her desk, in their small study, writing nothing. She knew she should be sensible and go to bed. She was achieving nothing and she would only be tired and irritable the next day, but she didn't move. It was the church clock striking three which finally roused her. Her fingers, holding the pen, still poised over the page, were stiff and white with cramp, and there were tight, painful knots of muscles in her shoulders, from her hunched position over the desk.

The final blow was that when she did eventually crawl into bed, some time after three am, she couldn't get to sleep. She felt exhausted but not sleepy, her mind still racing, like an overtuned engine, in its search for some way forward. What was it people said? Stories write themselves if you give yourself to them. Whoever said that had never tried to write a novel, she thought, with a wry bitterness. If anything, stories, or rather plots, were more like a maze; wherever you turned you found your way barred. To add to your humiliation, you could sometimes hear the voices of those who had been more successful, rejoicing in their speedy progress, while you stumbled from one blind alley to another.

Despite her exhaustion, she felt pleased with the analogy. It reflected so accurately the creative process, but not only that. In some ways, the last five years for her and Matthew had been just such a maze, moral and practical.

From the moment they had accepted they were in love, they had struggled to find a way forward. Some days every route seemed blocked; fear and shame can be formidable barriers and they both despaired. It was to their credit, she realised now, that they had gone on regardless. It would have been so much easier to give up, succumb to the gossip, the suspicion, the disgust. But they hadn't. And since their arrival in the gorge that way forward had been so much clearer. There was still the occasional blind alley, of course; problems over accommodation or employment, fear of discovery, and the inevitable personal tensions their situation was bound to throw up.

Rosalind sighed, as Matthew, stony-faced, his grin wiped away by her unpleasantness, cleared up the mess she had made; a perfect example of just that sort of tension, and on this occasion, it was all her fault.

When Matthew had disappeared back to the kitchen, without another word, and there was no more banging of doors and drawers, Rosalind slipped out of bed and went to the window. It was a lovely morning, one of summer's leftover days, determined not to let autumn encroach too soon. From a distance, at least, there was no sign yet of the leaves turning, although when they did Rosalind found herself falling in love with the place all over again. The rich reds, yellows, browns, and oranges, of the dying leaves was like a final farewell from the sun itself, a defiant blaze of colour to ward off the cold and wet. With autumn too, came the departure of the last, lingering, tourists as the village prepared to settle itself down for the quiet of winter. It had taken Rosalind and Matthew several years to get used to such a dramatic contrast between the summer and winter months. With the onset of autumn, the village seemed to turn in on itself, as an ancient melancholy descended, pushing it back in time. To begin with, they had both found such a change rather depressing, but as they learnt the act of retreating themselves, they began to adjust to the seasonal rhythm, and even welcomed it.

Despite September bringing Matthew a heavy teaching load, as his students got to grips with their new courses, he still tried to spend as much time on the river as he could. The days when he could kayak safely were coming to an end, and he wanted to make the most of every one of them. He loved the river as it got quieter and the visitors departed. Towards the end of September, there was hardly anyone on it in the late afternoons, and it was then, after school finished, that Matthew took to the water to revisit his favourite haunts one more time, before the river rose with the autumn rains, and cut him off from them.

At weekends, he would sometimes disappear all day, and although Rosalind was grateful for the time it gave her to write, there were some occasions when she felt aggrieved by how blithely he abandoned her for a rival love.

Standing at the window, soaking up the warmth of the still powerful sun, Rosalind guessed this weekend would be no different. She had to admit, if grudgingly, that such weather was too good to waste, although it would probably bring more people onto the river than Matthew expected at this time of the year.

To her surprise, however, he showed no sign of getting ready to go kayaking as the morning wore on. After she had dressed and had a yoghurt with Causse honey for breakfast, she found him already at his desk, in the study, hard at work on a batch of essays from his I.B. group.

'Aren't you going on the river today?' She asked, in a conciliatory tone, still feeling some remorse for her earlier ill humour.

'No. Not until later,' he replied, without looking up. 'And I was wondering if you might like to come too. There won't be many more chances.'

Rosalind, touched by the slightly hesitant tone in his voice, reached out and touched his cheek lightly with the back of her hand.

'Wouldn't you rather be on your own? I can struggle on with my writing.'

He must have sensed the grimace when she mentioned her writing, because he looked up with real concern on his face.

'Isn't it going well, the writing I mean? Can I help?'

Rosalind smiled, the last remnants of her irritation ebbing away as she replied.

'You've got enough to do with that mammoth pile of marking, but thanks for the offer.'

Peace had been restored and they both relaxed, as they contemplated the day ahead.

'Would you really like me to come?' Rosalind continued after a short pause. 'You're not just being nice to cheer me up?'

'Well, I am,' Matthew said laughing, 'but no, I really do want you to come. There's somewhere I want to show you, before we're banished for the winter.'

'That sounds intriguing,' Rosalind said happily, leaning forward to kiss him.

A trace of sweetness from the honey, still clung to her lips, and he returned the kiss, almost greedily, as if she too needed to be fully savoured while there was still time.

It was late afternoon before they went down to the river. Matthew had marked essays for the rest of the morning, while Rosalind tidied the flat and prepared the lunch. She was tempted to go back to her writing, but Matthew was against it.

'You need a break. You're trying too hard. Forget about it until tomorrow.'

He was probably right, and she hadn't the energy to

resist. Anyway, her best ideas often came when she was doing something else.

They had planned to have trout for lunch, one of their favourite meals, and she decided to make a special effort with the vegetables. Working in a hotel as a waitress over the last few years, she had picked up lots of tips on how to prepare and serve local dishes, and trout was one of the most popular. The secret lay in the sauce and the method of cooking, together with a generous dash of trial and error. According to Alain Grenier, proprietor and chief chef at the hotel, there was no recipe written down, it was just something you had to learn by watching and tasting.

'My father will never give away his secrets, you have to guess them,' Luc said one day, when they dropped in for lunch, not long after they had first arrived in the gorge. 'Even I don't know exactly how he gets that lovely crunchy texture in the skin of the trout, without over cooking or burning it. I think it's something to do with fine breadcrumbs sprinkled at just the right moment in the melted butter. You'll have to try yourself and keep trying until you get it right.'

And she had. Kept on trying, until even Luc, who had soon become a close friend, smacked his lips in approval, when she served him her own version of truite aux amandes. The almonds too had to have just the right degree of crispness, browned but not burnt, if they were to complement the succulent flesh of the trout, as it fell away from the bone.

Thinking back to those early days in the village, as she washed and gutted the trout, Rosalind was struck again by what a good friend Luc had been to them both.

Right from the beginning, it was Luc who had looked after them, when they first walked into his parents' hotel on that hot summer's day five years ago, and he was the one, who over the following weeks and months helped them to integrate and become part of the village community. He had found their first room for them and then, with the help of his father, the lovely, airy, flat she was now standing in. The offer of a job as waitress at the hotel had come next, a lifesaver in those early years, when they were struggling financially, and the only work Matthew could get was with the canoe company, based on the beach, close to the hotel. Rosalind was also sure that it was Luc's persistence which had finally helped Matthew secure his teaching post at the secondary school, temporary at first, but made permanent when Matthew proved his worth.

Putting the fish to one side, Rosalind started on the vegetables. She would try Alain's trick of cutting slices of courgette and tomato, and then interleaving them, so they formed parti-coloured vegetable cones, which could be doused in olive oil, and then baked in the oven. They went particularly well with trout, and Matthew loved them.

In retrospect, it was strange, if quite pleasing, how quickly the three of them had become close. It wasn't long before Matthew and Luc were behaving like brothers, sharing jokes and confidences, with an easy familiarity, which sometimes left Rosalind feeling quite jealous. With her, Luc was more restrained as if he needed to put a guard on his emotions. There was just one occasion when he let that guard slip, and it still made Rosalind uncomfortable to think about it.

It was a Friday, nearly three months after they had first arrived, and Luc had given her a lift into the nearest town, so that she could do a big shop. The car she and Matthew had hired had been returned weeks before, and they were dependent on Luc's kindness for lifts. Rosalind regretted giving up the car, but they couldn't afford to run it, and Matthew was also afraid it would make it too easy for others to trace their whereabouts.

Just occasionally, when the car had gone, Rosalind would experience a surge of panic at the thought that her means of escape had disappeared. She loved the gorge and the village as much as Matthew did, but it didn't stop her feeling trapped sometimes. There were days when the need to get up onto the Causse, and revel in its open wildness became overwhelming, and she felt a stirring of resentment at Matthew's eagerness to get rid of the car so promptly. If it hadn't been for Luc, and his willingness to play the chauffeur, she was convinced that this resentment, would eventually have turned into something more serious. Luc seemed aware of this possibility and did all he could to give her the moments of freedom he sensed she craved.

On this particular Friday, Luc had no big orders for the hotel to pick up, and so had stayed with Rosalind while she shopped. She usually found it irritating, having somebody hovering in the background watching every tiny decision she made, and as a result she and Matthew had had more trivial rows in supermarkets than almost anywhere else. With Luc, however, it was different. Interested as he was in the whole catering business, he took a more active role, suggesting new ingredients to spice up old recipes, and having a quick eye for the best fruit and vegetables. Like all French shoppers, he felt he had every right to handle the produce before he bought it, pressing the fruit and vegetables gently to test for freshness and ripeness.

After the shopping was done, they went for a coffee in a pleasant square, near the top of the town. It was mid-October, but on fine days, still warm enough to sit outside. Rosalind chose a table in the sun, while Luc went in to order the coffee. The square was very busy, as it was a popular meeting place for farmers from the Causse, and those living in the small villages along the gorge.

On the next table, two middle-aged women seemed in a celebratory mood, as they joked with the waiter and asked for a cognac with their coffee. They made no attempt to keep their voices down, and Rosalind soon gathered the cause of their jubilation. They had apparently opened a small shop in the gorge for the first time that season, and it had really taken off. From what Rosalind could make out it was in the next village to theirs, and sold mostly local produce, and fairly inexpensive jewellery, made from different types of rock common in the area. The women's delight in their success made Rosalind smile. It was good to think there were others who were also relishing their new life in the gorge, and she made a mental note to visit the shop when they were next in the village, which was some thirteen kilometres further south, and marked the beginning of the narrowest and most spectacular part of the gorge. Rosalind was also impressed by how fiercely independent and energetic the women appeared to be, with no sign of any men on the scene. One of them was English, with quite a pronounced Yorkshire accent, which made her heart thump uncomfortably in her chest, as her thoughts went back to the Haworth trip, and the beginning of it all. The women were fluent in both French and English, and the conversation seemed to veer between the two languages on a whim. In the French part, Rosalind tended to lose the thread a bit, as although her command of the language was gradually improving, it was still not much above GCSE level.

Engrossed in her involuntary eavesdropping, she had hardly registered Luc's return with their coffee, and he had to nudge her gently to get her attention.

Rosalind laughed, and then lowering her voice said, 'I got a bit caught up in –' and she moved her head slightly to indicate the next door table.

Luc nodded, as if he understood completely, barely glancing at the two women, who for some reason had suddenly fallen silent.

Rosalind had experienced this reaction to Luc before, but never quite so obviously. Wherever he went, the young man drew all eyes irresistibly towards him because of his striking good looks, and a natural gentleness and grace, which seemed to promise so much. Over the past few months, Rosalind had become used to his charm, but for a moment she saw it again, afresh, and she coloured slightly at the attention focused on them both.

Sipping their coffee, they chatted idly for a while about Luc's proposed improvements for the hotel. It had been a good season, and if he could persuade his parents, he wanted to plough a good proportion of the profits back into the business.

'You sound just like the two next door,' Rosalind said smiling. The women had already paid and left, casting envious glances at the handsome, young couple as they did so. Three farmers from the Causse took their place, one of whom acknowledged Luc with a quick nod, before he sat down.

'Do I?' replied Luc, with mock seriousness. 'Well I hope that's a compliment and not a criticism.'

'Yes, of course,' Rosalind said, feeling herself blush for no reason.

Luc looked at her sharply and then, without a word, leaned across the table and kissed her gently but firmly on the lips. For a few seconds, Rosalind found herself returning the pressure of his kiss with unexpected joy, before drawing back with embarrassment and confusion at the public nature of the gesture.

What was that for?' She said lightly, trying to restore some sense of the ordinary to the situation.

'I'm sorry. I shouldn't have done that,' Luc said calmly. 'Please forgive me. Blame my Latin temperament if you like.'

'It doesn't matter. Let's get going,' Rosalind said, excited and upset at the same time, and trying to hide her feelings in gathering up the bags of shopping, while Luc fished for a ten euro note to leave on the table.

They walked back to the car in silence, and although there was a distinct awkwardness between them on the journey home, by the time they began the descent into the gorge, a familiar sense of ease had begun to creep back into their conversation and they both gave an inward sigh of relief.

Putting two plates into the warming tray, Rosalind marvelled at how efficiently the incident had been disposed of. Neither of them had mentioned it again; it was as if it had never happened. For a while, they were a little more self-conscious than usual in each other's company, but then that too gradually disappeared, as the old relationship of warmth, tempered by a gallant restraint, returned. Matthew noticed nothing, and soon the whole incident seemed too trivial to mention, even in passing.

The lunch was a great success, and after they had finished eating, they sat for longer than usual over their wine. They both sensed that something about the day had changed for the better, although they couldn't have explained exactly what. Rosalind found she was really looking forward to their trip on the river, possibly the last of the season, and Matthew's slight air of mystery about it only added to the excitement. He seemed happy and on edge at the same time, as if fearful that she would be disappointed with the very thing he was so keen to share with her.

The afternoon was still warm, as they walked down through the village to the river. A few tourists still wandered the narrow, medieval, streets, but their numbers were diminishing quickly, as autumn approached. Soon most of the small shops would shut their doors, the unsold stock packed away for another year, their owners often disappearing to their winter homes in local towns. The permanent population was no more than a few hundred and that number was dropping steadily every year.

Discussing this worrying decline with Luc, Matthew was glad to feel they were doing their own small bit to reverse the trend.

'If only more people like you would come and settle here,' Luc sad wistfully, 'the village might have a chance then. It's new blood we need, we haven't enough of our own.'

Matthew had to agree. In discussion with his own senior students, he was only too aware that their hopes were set on a life and career far away from the village, even if their hearts were left behind.

With the coming of autumn, a gentle quiet would descend on the village as it was reclaimed by a past, never really out of sight. For Rosalind that was one of the greatest charms of the place, as she let her mind run back through the centuries, repopulating the village with its very earliest inhabitants. She imagined them building the first, rough, dwellings, close to the river, before expanding gradually up the side of the gorge, as they tried to gain a toe-hold in such a wild and secret place. Some sense of that secrecy, of being hidden away from prying eyes, still lingered in the narrow alleys and tiny courtyards which held the village together, a haphazard structure, clinging to the rock face. Her imaginings came into sharper focus when she heard the story of the Saint, who had founded the abbey in the seventh century, and given her name to the village.

Only a small part of the abbey still survived, a lofty, barn-like structure, its walls made from large blocks of limestone hewed out from the great bluffs of rock, which gave the gorge its distinctive grandeur. Rosalind guessed it might have been the refectory, where the nuns ate their simple meals in quiet contemplation, as there was no sign of the decoration and religious iconography which might denote an abbey church. There was a disturbing atmosphere in the place, however, but it wasn't one of prayerful devotion. Instead it seemed redolent of unspoken thoughts and desires, long suppressed by discipline and duty.

Rosalind would often pause for a few minutes in the ancient building, when she walked up to the secondary school which adjoined it, to meet Matthew at the end of the school day, or to do a few hours clerical work in the school office. On these occasions, her own unexpressed feelings would seem strangely at home in the cavernous building, as if somebody understood, had been there before, and she always left the building reassured and a little more at peace with herself. Matthew agreed that the place had an unusual atmosphere, but refused to take her feelings seriously, teasing her gently, with an amused scepticism.

'Do you think one of the nuns, or even the abbess herself is trying to communicate with you?' he asked one day, when she seemed particularly caught up in the spirit of the place. 'I doubt if you would have made a very convincing nun, too independent by half, not to say sexy.'

To his surprise, Rosalind replied quite seriously, ignoring his humorous jibe.

'It's not that exactly. It's more to do with being recognised, rather than accepted—-treading the same path—something like that—I don't know, it's difficult to explain.'

And in the end she gave up trying, and instead stored her impressions of the abbey, and her thoughts about its founder, at the back of her mind, where she put all the oddments, which one day, might give her a story to tell.

Reaching the narrow street, which ran parallel to the main road bordering the river, Matthew stopped at the dark entrance to a small shop, to pick up a paddle he had left for repair. Waiting for him, Rosalind gazed down the long street, one of the few straight ones in the village. It was empty now of the makeshift stands displaying goods to tempt the tourist, making it easier for her to imagine it in medieval times. Then it was the chief thoroughfare through the village, where the horses and wagons of itinerant traders would make their way, with some difficulty, through its narrow confines, on their journey south through the gorge, and on to the nearest seaport. They would have had stories to tell, Rosalind thought wistfully, but now all lost, as if they were nothing. With this reflection, came a spontaneous loosening of ideas in her own mind, and she suddenly felt much more optimistic about finding a way out of her own blind alley. Matthew's advice was good; she did need a break, time to let her imagination go free, and a few hours on the river might just give her that space.

The two kayaks were identical, except for their colour. Rosalind's was blue, and Matthew's yellow, shading off to white on their undersides. They had been specially made for them by a firm in Clermont Ferrand the year before, and were particularly light and easy to manoeuvre on the fast flowing stretches of the river. At first, Rosalind queried such unnecessary expense, but she changed her mind completely once she was on the water. Both of them had become good kayakers over the previous few years, although Matthew's many extra hours on the river had given him such a detailed knowledge of its vagaries, that he could negotiate the trickiest rapid with a skill and confidence, which left Rosalind exclaiming in admiration. She didn't want to rival him; the river was his thing, and she felt a genuine pride and delight in his expertise.

The river was already in shadow, when they pushed off from the rocky beach near the hotel. They had put a flask of tea and some sandwiches into Matthew's barrel, as well as their sweaters for when the evening got cooler. Matthew had indicated they would be on the river for several hours, but he still wouldn't say exactly where they were headed.

The first stretch of river was easy to navigate, and they sculled along side by side, enjoying the quiet. There were a few other kayakers on the river but as time passed, they melted away, their voices fading, like those of children called in from play. Sun still lit the upper rock faces, as if they were the setting for some grand experiment in son et lumière, but on the river itself dusk was deepening all the time.

When they approached a short rapid, Matthew would take the lead, guiding his kayak skilfully between large rocks, until he judged the moment was right to let it go with the race of water, only using his paddle again, if the kayak came too near the looming rock faces, under which the river swirled with devilish energy. Rosalind would wait for Matthew to reach the calmer water beyond the rapid, before she too followed the same path through the rocks, and released her kayak to the power of the current. In the fading light, the foaming water laced the darkness of the river with swirls and streamers of eerie whiteness, like some extreme fairground ride. Both of them loved the feeling of the ebullient river, carrying them forward with such speed and energy, and Rosalind shrieked out loud in her excitement, in contrast to Matthew's disciplined control.

'Professional kayakers don't do that,' he told her sternly. 'You sound like a kid on the big wheel.'

Rosalind just laughed, promised not to do it again, and then promptly broke her promise at the next rapid they came to.

'I give up. You're hopeless,' Matthew said, laughing too, the joy in her eyes catching at his heart.

It was almost seven by the time they reached the next village, and it wouldn't be long before dusk turned to night.

'It's not far now,' Matthew said encouragingly, as they slid their kayaks over the weir, just north of the village, and scrambled down to retrieve them from the deep pool below. 'It won't take us much more than half an hour from here.'

Rosalind nodded. 'It had better be good after all this—your surprise. At this rate I'll be too exhausted to enjoy it.'

They almost missed it. In the near dark, stretches of the river looked so similar, even Matthew was upon the place before he realised it. Swinging his kayak abruptly to the right, he called to Rosalind, who was a short way behind, to do the same. Looking up, there was only a narrow strip of sky visible as the sheer slabs of rock came together in the narrowest part of the gorge, and it was towards one of these giant rock faces that Matthew directed his kayak, until he felt the bottom scrape on a shelving bank of shingle, and he could jump out and haul the kayak clear of the river. Matthew unstrapped the barrel and then helped Rosalind pull her kayak alongside his.

They stood side by side, gazing up at a great fissure in the rock, which at the bottom widened out to form a cave, dry and sandy, and going deep into the side of the gorge.

'Welcome,' Matthew said softly. 'Please come inside.'

'Have I been here before?' Rosalind asked, reaching for Matthew's hand, like a child afraid of the dark.

'No. I think I pointed it out to you once or twice, but you've never stopped here. I thought it was time you did.'

As he spoke, he led her further into the cave, towards two large rocks, embedded in the sand, and so positioned to form an ideal place to store things.

Letting go of Rosalind's hand, Matthew knelt down on the sand and pulled out a black, plastic bag from a natural recess under one of the rocks.

' Here we have everything madam might need,' he said smiling up at Rosalind, whose face was a pale disc in the gloom.

He got to his feet and pulled a picnic rug from the bag, which he spread on the sand, pulling the top of it into the angle made by the two rocks.

'And now let there be light.'

He switched on a small, bright, torch, which was next out of the bag, and immediately the cave was alive with dancing shadows, which glided and twisted over the limestone. Sweeping the cave with the light, it seemed to change in shape and size before their eyes, as if reluctant to give up its secrets, in the face of such intrusion.

'What a place,' breathed Rosalind, her voice swallowed up in the vastness of the cave. 'You would never think it was this big from outside.'

That's the magic of it,' Matthew said, just as quietly. 'And that's what I wanted to share.'

His fingers touched hers, as she turned towards him, and he pulled her down quickly onto the rug beside him. Feeling her trembling, he held her very close for a few minutes. No sound entered the cave, except for the faint sigh of tiny waves breaking on the shingle bank, as the strengthening breeze ruffled the surface of the river, bringing a few brown trout hopefully to the surface.

Their lovemaking was tender but intense. Neither of them cried out, although their bodies ached with the desire which had wrenched them, brutally and ruthlessly, from the known and loved, to cast them up on the sandy floor of a cave, the strange detritus of an uncaring river.

PART THREE

I. Maggie

In January 1974 Maggie suddenly disappeared, without trace, as if spirited away by some unknown force. At least that's how it appeared to her friends at the time. She had just completed her first term in the Lower Sixth, and was generally regarded as a bright student, university bound. She was studying English Literature, History, and Latin, but was still undecided about which subject to pursue to degree level. Her first love, the one she regarded as recreation rather than work, was English Literature but she was equally good at all three. Her parents, neither of whom had been to university themselves, were prepared to leave the choice to her. They were stoutly working class and proud of it, and as long as there was a respectable job at the end of it, they were content.

From the day Maggie started at the local grammar school, her parents had done their best to support her. In their eyes, that meant encouraging her to do everything the school asked of her, to the best of her ability, and without fuss or complaint. If occasionally Maggie moaned about a teacher being unfair, or too hard on her, she got little sympathy from either of her parents. Her father would simply raise his eyebrows and say firmly, 'it's for your own good. They know what's best. Just get on with it.' Maggie soon realised that her parents had a blind trust in teachers, which always rendered them right in their eyes, and if she wanted to fight any battles, she would have to do it on her own.

During her first five years in the school, things went fairly smoothly for Maggie. She had a small group of good friends, who tended to look to her for leadership, because of her lively, independent, nature. She wasn't bossy, her natural sensitivity making her too aware of others' feelings for that, but she knew her own mind, and was fiercely loyal to her friends.

From her very earliest years, Maggie never wanted to miss a day of school.

She hated the thought of things going on while she was away, and she would always struggle to school, if she possibly could. Once or twice, when she was running a high temperature, her mother insisted she stay in bed, and Maggie spent the whole day wondering how every lesson was going, and what her friends were doing and saying. As an only child, she was quite used to her own company, but on days when she should have been at school and wasn't, she rebelled against the isolation, feeling abandoned and left out. Her mother would make a fuss of her, bringing her poached egg on mashed potato, and a magazine from the local shop, but it didn't help much. She still felt lonely, cast adrift, and so sometimes, even when she felt really ill, she badgered her mother to let her return to school for the afternoon session.

It was the quietness of the house which unsettled her the most. Her father left for work very early, just before six, to cycle to the timber yard on the other side of town, where he had just been promoted to foreman. Her mother, after the chores of the day had been done, settled to her sewing. She didn't have a job which took her from the house, but was employed by a local dress shop to do any alterations which customers required. She was a highly skilled seamstress, although with no formal training, apart from a short course, one day a week for six weeks, which she had attended at the local community centre before Maggie was born. She made all her own clothes, as well as her daughter's, although when she was growing up Maggie didn't always appreciate her mother's skill. When she started at the grammar school, she longed to have a shop-bought skirt, and a white, poplin, blouse like the other girls, but her mother insisted on making both. The skirt was just about acceptable to Maggie, but the blouse, beautifully tailored out of cream Viyella, seemed like a garment from another era, and warm and comfortable though it was, Maggie hated it. She never mentioned how strongly she felt but her mother must have guessed eventually. By the time Maggie reached the third form, her mother had agreed to buy the uniform from the local department store. On their return with the new skirts and blouses, she went quickly upstairs to Maggie's bedroom, removed the Viyella blouses from the drawer, and calmly tore them into several pieces, suitable for cleaning and polishing cloths. For years afterwards, Maggie could never open the cleaning cupboard without an aching sense of guilt at the sight of her mother's exquisite handiwork, reduced to rags, and stuffed in a box with other old cloths and half-finished tins of polish, dried and cracked around the edges.

On some of these infrequent days of illness, Maggie's mother would bring her sewing and the radio upstairs, and for a while the day, although still different, wouldn't seem quite so empty. Grateful for her mother's company, Maggie would talk to her a little about what went on at school, careful to select only those things she knew her mother would understand and approve. For example, she never mentioned boys, although by the time she reached the third form they were most definitely on the scene. Looking back it was obvious that her growing disgust with homemade uniform had quite a lot to do with the increasing importance of boys in her life, although neither could be admitted openly.

Towards the end of the third year, she had just turned fourteen, one boy in particular caught her attention. She saw him first on the train, in his navy cadet uniform. The grammar school she attended was in a town, some fifteen miles from her home, and her journey to school every day involved car, train, and bus. When she passed the eleven plus, her father gave up his bike and bought a secondhand, yellow and white, Ford Prefect so he could run her to the station each morning. In the afternoon, she would catch the bus back, as her father was still at work, and her mother couldn't or wouldn't drive. Maggie was never quite sure which.

Lots of boys and girls got on the train at the same station as Maggie, as four, large, secondary schools were in the neighbouring town. The two grammar schools were single sex, and a mile apart, and they were mirrored by two technical high schools, also single sex, and in different parts of the town.

The boy in the cadet uniform went to the grammar school; there was no CCF at the technical high school. He must have been at least fifteen when she first noticed him, as the boys were not eligible to join the CCF until the fourth year. From a very young age, Maggie had been fascinated by the sea and ships, so the naval uniform only added to the attraction. He was relatively short for his age, only an inch or two taller than Maggie herself, but it was his complexion which made him stand out. Unlike the other spotty youths who crowded onto the train, his skin was wonderfully smooth, and clear, and lightly tanned, as if he had just returned from a holiday on the Costa Brava.

Getting into the same compartment one morning, Maggie couldn't take her eyes off him. He was with a group of friends, and although he joined in their conversations every now and then, he obviously preferred to sit quietly and gaze out of the window. When it was time to get off the train, he lingered behind the others, catching Maggie's eye for a moment, and smiling shyly as he stepped down onto the platform. Maggie blushed and hastily finished repacking her bag which had fallen off the seat when the train stopped suddenly, dumping its contents on the floor. By the time she was on the platform, the boy had already disappeared, and she walked the last half mile to school, in a state of excited disappointment she had never felt before.

During the day, she could think of nothing but the journey home. Usually so eager and attentive in class, she found her mind wandering, even in those subjects she liked the best. The only time she felt able to concentrate fully on her work was in English.

For their novel they were studying Jane Eyre and had been asked for homework to read and think about the passage in chapter twelve where Jane meets Rochester for the first time. Conscientious as always, Maggie had done her work thoroughly, her imagination caught immediately by the highly charged and romantic nature of the encounter. She had diligently made careful notes of her first impressions in her rough book, linking them to appropriate quotations as they had been taught to do by their English teacher, Miss Winthrop. When the lesson arrived, last in the morning, she couldn't wait to hear the views of her teacher and fellow pupils on the passage. Her own brief encounter on the train that morning had changed everything. No words had been uttered, nothing had really happened, but something had begun, just as it had for Jane and Rochester, in that wintry lane, on the road to Hay.

Miss Winthrop always made quite an entrance when she came into class, sweeping her long, fair, hair away from her face, and hitching her gown higher on her shoulders, as she greeted her pupils. Maggie loved Miss Winthrop, with the suffocating passion of which only fourteen year old girls are capable, and she always felt a slight tightening in her chest when her beloved mistress entered the classroom.

To begin the lesson, Miss Winthrop read the passage again, her warm, rich, voice investing Bronte's description with an emotional energy, which brought the text alive, for even the dullest of her students. For Maggie, the words leapt off the page, as if freshly written. The piercing cold made her shudder, and she too started with fear at a rush under the hedge, and the sudden appearance of dog and rider, whose steed slid from under him on the glistening sheet of ice. With Jane, she too hastened to the stranger's rescue, undeterred by his brusqueness and imperious tone. His very gruffness attracted her, as did his brooding, dark, looks. With Jane, she answered his questions and helped him remount his horse, strangely glad to be of assistance to one so ungracious in his manner.

Pulling herself out of the scene, with an almost physical effort, as Bronte's words penetrated her consciousness with new meaning, Maggie listened with pounding heart to the last paragraph of the reading.

'It was an incident of no moment, no romance, no interest in a sense, yet it marked with change one single hour of a monotonous life.'

The words were meant for her, what had happened to her that morning, it all fitted. The words were meant for her. They must be.

She didn't see him on the train that afternoon. There were some boys in CCF uniform, but no navy cadets. She sat by the window so she could watch for late arrivals on the platform, but he didn't appear. She was bitterly disappointed but she had to hide it. So far she had told no one about the boy, not even her best friend Heather, who travelled on the train too, getting off one stop before Maggie, and cycling the rest of the way home. Sometimes Maggie would go with her and stay overnight. Heather's house was noisy and chaotic, full of small boys, and the complete opposite to the quiet order of Maggie's home. Both girls enjoyed doing homework together, as they were good at different subjects and could help each other out. Maggie would often write out an English essay in rough for Heather, while her friend whipped through some simultaneous equations for her. They saw nothing wrong with the arrangement educationally, it seemed the intelligent thing to do, sharing talents to the advantage of both. If their teachers suspected anything, nothing was said, and as long as the homework was actually done, their parents didn't interfere.

Once the boy came on the scene, Maggie became more reluctant to stay at her friend's house, and had to explain why. Heather said she understood, but was secretly rather upset at being put in second place to someone Maggie hadn't even spoken to. The friendship between the two girls cooled for a bit, as Heather waited for her friend to come to her senses. She knew how passionate Maggie could be in her obsessions, and that there was no point in trying to argue her out of it. Time would put things right eventually, she hoped.

For Maggie, things weren't going too well either. It was a week before she caught sight of the boy again, and then it was only a fleeting glimpse. Getting off the train, on the way home, there he was, in school uniform this time, just reaching the top of the steps leading to the footbridge. She pushed her way through the crowd of milling schoolchildren in an effort to catch up with him, but it was no good. When she reached the top of the steps herself, he was nowhere to be seen. It almost seemed as if he was avoiding her, but she knew that couldn't be so. Most probably he wasn't thinking about her at all.

The following week Heather asked her to stay on the Tuesday night but she refused. She felt a bit foolish but wouldn't give in. The one day she wasn't there he would be, and she couldn't risk it. Tuesday came and went without incident, and when she met Heather on the train the following morning, Maggie hanging out of the window to call to her friend as usual, her face said it all. Across the crowded compartment Heather mouthed, 'I told you so,' and Maggie turned away, angry and embarrassed.

During the day she tried to push all thoughts of the boy from her mind. In English she concentrated on her feelings for Miss Winthrop, which had lost some of their intensity since the boy, but in other lessons it wasn't quite so easy to distract herself.

It was a relief when four o'clock came.

Feeling both foolish and fed up, Maggie made no effort to look out for the boy on the way home. She didn't even hurry for the usual train, but waited for Heather who had gone to check the hockey fixtures for the Colts XI, and caught the later one. The rush was over, and they had a compartment to themselves. Heather suggested getting on with some homework and Maggie agreed. It was three stops until Heather's station, they had plenty of time.

Twenty minutes later, they were so absorbed in each other's homework, Heather nearly missed her stop. Grabbing her books off Maggie and bundling everything into her bag, she shouted at Maggie to open the door. Tumbling onto the platform, she nearly collided with someone trying to enter the compartment. In her confusion she failed to register who it was, but as the train pulled away from the station, she could see both occupants quite clearly. And one of them was the boy.

It was months before they went on a proper date. To begin with they were just happy to meet on the train, often waiting for the later one on their way home, so as to have the chance of a compartment to themselves. The boy's name was Mark and he was in the fifth form, his O-Level year, as he told Maggie proudly. His family had moved into the area quite recently and he had started at the grammar school the previous September. His childhood was spent in Dartmouth, where he was born and where he had gained his love of everything to do with the sea and ships. A navy cadet in the CCF was a poor substitute for what he had had before, but it was better than nothing.

'What did you have before?' Maggie asked curiously, not long after their first meeting.

'Well, I had my own boat for a start, which I could sail when and where I liked,' he said slowly, glancing at Maggie, to gauge her reaction, 'but don't get me wrong, it wasn't as grand as it sounds. During the summer, after my ninth birthday, my father and I built the boat together. It wasn't much bigger than a dinghy, but very fast and light, and I loved it. My father believes in people learning their craft the hard way, and he said if I wanted to be a proper sailor, I needed to know my boat inside out. And he was right. I have never learnt so much, so quickly, anywhere else.'

Maggie was impressed. Mark's words could have sounded like a boast, but they didn't. He was too open and direct for that, qualities which Maggie at fourteen had already learnt to admire. In another conversation, some weeks later, he told her that he intended to join the navy after university.

'I shall go back to my roots,' he said in such a grown up way, that he suddenly seemed a lot older than his fifteen years. 'I want to enter The Royal Naval College at Dartmouth on the graduate entry scheme. It's been my dream since I was a kid.'

It couldn't have been better. Everything about the boy was perfect, or almost. He could do with being a little taller but that would come in time. He probably hadn't had his growth spurt yet, Maggie reflected. They had done quite a lot about the development of the adolescent in Biology recently, amid the usual nervous titters and sidelong glances. There were no separate sex education lessons, it was all down to the biology teacher to cover that sort of stuff. Maggie's knowledge was still rather patchy, but she was reluctant to ask her parents to fill in the gaps. They would have answered her questions, but they wouldn't have felt comfortable doing it. There were certain things you didn't talk about in her family and sex was certainly one of them. Death was another. If you didn't talk about them, they didn't exist and life was easier for everyone.

During these early assignations on the train, all they did was talk. Hearts were pounding and hands were clammy but they didn't touch. From an early age Maggie had heard her mother speak with such disgust of girls who were too forward for their own good. She had only just begun to understand what her mother meant, and it filled her with dread. One false move, and Mark might regard her with contempt for ever. Sometimes, however, when they did manage to get an empty compartment, which wasn't all that often, she did feel it was a bit of a waste. She sensed that Mark felt the same, but neither of them had the courage to do anything. Talking, not even hand holding, were as far as things were allowed to go, for what seemed weeks and weeks.

It was their first proper date which changed things a bit. In itself it wasn't a particularly happy or enjoyable experience, and years later Maggie would look back on the occasion with considerable compassion for her fourteen year old self.

To begin with she had to tell her parents and they didn't really approve.

'You are too young to be going on a date,' her father said sternly. 'You should be concentrating on school work, not thinking about boys.'

His reaction was predictable and it got worse.

'Where are you going on this date and when?' he went on, as if he were interrogating her about some crime she was about to commit.

'Only the local flicks on Friday,' she replied casually. 'There's a romantic comedy we'd both like to see.'

'Well, I'll take you and pick you up,' her father said firmly. 'You're not coming back on the bus, on your own, at that time of night.'

Maggie's heart sank.

'I'm sure Mark will see me home,' she said desperately. 'You don't need to worry Dad.'

It was no good. Her father was adamant. Instead of anticipation and excitement, there would be humiliation and embarrassment. The whole evening was going to be a disaster.

It wasn't quite as bad as that, but it was awkward. Mark said he understood but she could tell he was hurt that her parents didn't trust him.

They got seats on the back row, as lovers usually do, but they were right in the middle, and they had to squeeze past other giggling couples to reach them. Mark had offered to buy Maggie sweets or popcorn, but she didn't want any. Her throat was dry, and she felt vaguely nauseous at the thought of food.

During the advertisements, they sat rigidly, side by side, eyes glued to the screen but taking nothing in, elbows occasionally touching, as if by accident.

Just before the main feature started, the screen went black, and they were plunged into even deeper gloom. Maggie felt Mark shift uneasily on his seat, as a ripple of excitement passed along the back row, and then he grasped her hand, pulling it onto his lap, as they both gazed fixedly ahead. Maggie could hardly breathe, their hands locked in a sweaty embrace, she found slightly unpleasant. When the film started and the gloom lightened, she pulled her hand away gently, rubbing it surreptitiously on her jeans to remove the dampness.

Mark made no further attempt to retrieve her hand, but when they were both laughing helplessly at one of the funniest moments in the film, he suddenly turned towards her and she felt his lips, dry and warm, brush hers, full of tentative longing, but afraid to do more. And for a moment her heart sang.

They watched the rest of the film in a daze, which was brutally shattered an hour later, when they caught sight of Maggie's father waiting for them in the foyer.

They never went on a date like that again. By mutual agreement, they decided to keep their friendship well away from the prying eyes of parents, and for the next two years they only met on the train, or in town after school, or on official school activities. They rarely saw each other at weekends, although they did telephone sometimes, if they were sure they wouldn't be overheard.

Despite its unsatisfactory nature, the cinema visit was a watershed of sorts. It made them aware that they wanted to be more than friends, if not then, eventually. They felt an excitement in each other's company which was lacking in other friendships, and they wanted to keep it to themselves. Maggie told Heather a few things, but not much. About the most important thing, what she felt about Mark, the connection between them, she said nothing. It was difficult to understand it fully herself, and to talk about it would have seemed disloyal. Even at fourteen, Maggie had strong opinions about quite a lot of things, and loyalty was one of them. Admittedly, not being totally open with her best friend wasn't easy either, and she felt a real sense of loss as their friendship became less close. Maggie was sensible enough, however, to know that her problems weren't unique, they were just part of growing up, as they were continually being told in PSHE. But they still felt unique and they still hurt.

Despite the intensity of their friendship, and its importance to both of them, it still had to fit round school. They were both hard workers, enthusiastic about their studies, and quite ambitious for their futures. Mark did well at O Level, as expected, and in the September after they first met, he embarked on four A Levels. He was a good all-rounder, but his interest in a naval career meant that he was advised to stick to the Sciences and Maths. Like Maggie, however, he was also an avid reader, and had done extremely well in English Literature. It was one of the things which had really cemented their friendship, a passion for books. So often, it enabled them to talk about ideas and feelings which were difficult to approach more directly. Behind the protection of a novel, play or poetry, they felt free to explore their own doubts and fears, joy and desire, with a confidence and maturity which surprised them both.

With Maggie's encouragement, Mark decided to make his fourth A-Level English Literature. There were a few raised eyebrows from his parents and teachers but they didn't stop him. By then, more students were beginning to do a mixture of Arts and Science subjects, and so his choice didn't appear too odd. Maggie was delighted. She had already decided that English Literature would be one of her chosen subjects when the time came, and Mark's decision seemed to confirm something important about their friendship. Despite a hesitant start, they enjoyed kissing and holding hands, but they wanted more than just a physical connection. Maggie's friends, apart from Heather who simply dismissed boys as a nuisance, frequently dropped hints about their latest sexual adventures, sniggering over articles in rather dubious magazines, and giving each other meaningful looks. Maggie kept herself aloof from such febrile discussions, anxious to keep her romantic illusions intact. Occasionally, an overheard remark would both arouse and disgust her, even as she doubted its truth. She asked Mark once what his friends said about the girls they knew, but he was reluctant to say much.

'You don't want to know. It can be quite crude and juvenile, and mostly lies I expect.'

He sounded angry and blushed slightly as he spoke, so Maggie didn't pursue it.

During the spring and summer, when the days were longer, and the weather better, they would often meet at a small cafe by the river, and walk for an hour or so, along the towpath. They would each give the same excuse at home; they needed to work in the library, or there was a talk at school they had to go to. Neither of them liked lying, but they both agreed it was necessary.

'If they knew we were meeting so often, they would only think the worst,' Mark said one afternoon in early May, towards the end of his Lower Sixth year. They had stopped to watch three swans gliding effortlessly downstream, as if they owned the river.

'I know,' Maggie laughed. 'They would never believe we spend all our time just talking about books, rather than snogging in the bushes.'

'Would you rather do that?' Mark said abruptly, turning away to look fixedly at the swans, disappearing rapidly round a bend in the river.

'No, of course not. Our friendship is more than just that, I hope,' Maggie said stoutly. 'And if that makes us odd, so be it.'

Maggie's defiance made Mark smile, and linking hands, they continued their walk.

There were moments, of course, when books weren't enough, and those moments became more and more frequent as time passed. To hold hands, to kiss, became torture, as desire called for so much more. Unprepared and proud, they struggled to control their feelings, but they couldn't always manage it.

On one occasion, travelling home on the late train, alone in a compartment, between stations, Mark had kissed her breasts. They were sitting by the window, facing each other, when he leaned across the aisle and began to unbutton her white, school blouse. Gazing at him solemnly, she made no attempt to push his hand away, but instead pushed her bra cups down a little so that more of her breasts were exposed. Moving off the seat, Mark knelt on the floor in front of her. He kissed both breasts gently, again and again, until Maggie pulled him so close his face was crushed against her warm skin, and he could feel them both trembling.

That day the next station saved them, but they both knew a day would come when nothing would.

At the end of June 1973, there was a big Leavers' party organised by a joint committee, made up of students from the fifth and upper sixth years in the two grammar schools.

It was to be held at the boys' school, as they owned a huge marquee which could be erected on the playing fields, and accommodated five hundred quite comfortably. Tickets were sold on a first come, first served, basis but at twenty pounds a head were too expensive for some students.

Mark and Maggie were keen to go, and Mark insisted on paying for Maggie's ticket. To begin with, she refused to accept the offer, saying that it was far too much for him to spend in one evening.

'It's not,' he said stubbornly. 'This is a special occasion. We have both just finished exams, I'm leaving school, you will soon be a sixth former. We have to celebrate. Anyway I have plenty in my savings account.'

Maggie gave in. When Mark was really determined, there was no opposing him. Typical of his natural modesty, he had also forgotten to mention that he had gained a place to read Marine Engineering at Southampton, a very competitive course, which he had done extremely well to get a place on. For the moment, Maggie was refusing to think about what would happen when Mark disappeared off the scene. There was no way she would be able to travel down to Southampton to see him on a regular basis, and he certainly wouldn't have the money to come home all that often. They both avoided the subject, afraid that if they talked about it, it would become the reality neither of them wanted to accept.

Their last exams were only a few days before the party, so fortunately they had plenty to occupy their minds and little time to brood. Maggie's main concern, once her last paper, Latin set books, was over, was what she was going to wear. The party was formal, even though there would be a disco, not a band, and the boys were expected to wear at least a suit, if not a dinner jacket. Maggie knew that nearly all the other girls would be in long dresses and she hadn't got one, at least not one she was prepared to be seen in. She did have her bridesmaid dress, which she'd worn at her cousin's wedding the previous summer, but it was probably already too small, and certainly didn't have the sophisticated look required for the Leavers'party. There were an awkward few minutes when her mother offered to run something up for her, but the look on Maggie's face must have alerted her to her daughter's feelings, and she quickly dropped the idea. In the end, and only two days before the actual event, Maggie found a black, halter neck, dress on the sale rack, in the local department store. It was thirty pounds, reduced from sixty, and fitted her perfectly. Her father said she deserved it after all her efforts in the exams. Mark had his interview suit, which he was quite happy to wear, but Maggie begged him to hire a dinner jacket.

'For me, just this once. It will go so well with my dress. And you will look so handsome,' she added teasingly.

Mark, aware that they were heading rapidly towards the end of something, finally agreed. It seemed the least he could do.

Looking back at the Leavers' party some months later, when her whole world had been turned on its head, it was clear to Maggie that there was a certain inevitability to what happened that evening which nothing could have stopped.

They met at the station and caught the 7.10 train. Maggie's father had offered to drive them to Mark's school, but they had turned him down. An unspoken desire to be free of all parental control united them, and added to the excitement of the evening. They made a handsome couple as they waited on the platform, part of and yet also distinct from, the chattering group of students, catching the train with them. Maggie looked beautiful in her new, black dress, much older than her sixteen years, with her hair fastened back in a black, velvet, bow and a dark red wrap, flung carelessly round her shoulders. Mark, who at sixteen had been quite short for his age, now topped six feet, his strong, slender, frame already giving him the bearing of a proud, naval officer. It was not only their striking good looks which caused heads to turn, but something about how they were together. The connection between them was palpable, and for those who knew them well, disturbing. Friends wondered how they would bear the separation which was bound to come, their closeness so much more than the animal attraction, which had brought most couples together. Friends openly referred to them as soul mates, out of a genuine respect, tinged with envy.

Maggie and Mark had gone out to very few social occasions as a couple, so when they did, they caused a stir.

It was generally agreed by everyone who attended it that the Leavers' party was a success. The disco was good, the food plentiful, and the fruit cup acceptable. A few bold, fifth form, boys smuggled in some forbidden bottles of vodka and gin, and a number of girls got hideously drunk but the staff on duty coped, and the whole business went unnoticed by most.

Towards the end of the evening, the disco was due to pack up at midnight, Chris, one of Mark's friends from cadets, suggested some of them went back to his house and continue the party there. Mark was reluctant, but Maggie beginning to tire of the school surroundings, jumped at the idea.

Chris' house was only a ten minute walk from the school and although it was 11.30, the night was still very warm. The girls were radiant from the heat of the marquee, and the frenetic dancing, and most of the boys had discarded their jackets and loosened the collars of their dress shirts. A group of twelve, including Mark and Maggie, had accepted Chris' invitation, and their high spirits echoed down the quiet suburban streets, causing a few curtains to twitch, at such a late disturbance. Passing a small supermarket at the end of Chris' road, they were surprised to see the lights still on, and the door open. A few boys went in to look for drink, while the rest trailed down the road behind Chris and his girlfriend Jo, chattering and laughing, in small groups.

Maggie and Mark walked slightly apart from the others, hands linked and talking quietly. Mark felt a little uneasy at leaving the party, but Chris had promised to ring parents when they got to his house, and explain the change of plan.

'You can get a taxi home from my place, instead of the station,' he said reassuringly. 'It will be fine, you'll see.'

Mark was fairly sure Maggie's parents wouldn't approve, but he went along with it all the same. He knew Maggie didn't want the evening to end, and neither did he.

Chris' house was in darkness when they arrived. His parents were away for a few days, visiting his sister, who was married with a young child, and lived in Cumbria. According to Mark, they were quite happy for him to bring a few friends home after the party. He had called them earlier from the school to check. If it had been anyone else no-one would have believed him, but Chris was a quiet, straightforward, boy who everyone trusted. Mark was just surprised that he had been bold enough to ask them all back in the first place, it wasn't really in character. Perhaps the answer lay in the evening itself, which had its own strange atmosphere, full of suppressed longings, daring thoughts, and the thrilling tension of the unknown. Mark sensed an unfamiliar recklessness in himself, and as they gathered in a group behind Chris who was fumbling with the front door lock in the dark, he whispered to Maggie, releasing her hand and slipping his arm round her waist.

'I don't want to go inside again yet. Let's explore the garden.'

A murmured 'Yes' as Maggie's lips brushed his cheek in a light caress, set his heart thudding. He grasped her hand so tightly, that she gave a little yelp of pain, but offered no resistance as he led round the side of the house, and towards a small stand of trees, at the far side of an extensive lawn. Lights came on in the house but the darkness under the trees was too thick for any light to penetrate. Above the canopy of leaves, the sky was clear, and stars shone wickedly in the deep blue of a midsummer sky.

The consequences of the evening were unlucky, but not unlikely. By the time Maggie's pregnancy was finally confirmed, Mark was already well settled at Southampton and she had started on her A Levels. To begin with, she told no one about her missed periods, refusing to accept what she knew was true. The morning sickness was harder to ignore, but she often just felt nauseous and wasn't actually sick, which made it a little easier to conceal. It was Heather who eventually tackled her on the subject and persuaded her to buy a kit from Boots. The friends had become close again since Mark's departure, and were spending a lot of time together as before. When the test came out positive, Heather begged her friend to tell her parents.

'They have to know Maggie,' she pleaded. 'Things have to be decided. Arrangements made. You have to tell them.'

So she did. Tell them. And they were shocked as she expected them to be. But not angry. They loved her too much for that. She wanted to tell Mark but they said no. Better not. They were too young for marriage, so what was the point? Maggie, confused and miserable, did what she was told as her parents took charge.

With the agreement of her head teacher, Mrs Dulwich,

Maggie was to be allowed to stay at school until she started to show, but then she would have to leave. Staff who taught her, would be asked to provide work so she could continue her studies on her own, but they would not be told the reason for her absence. Maggie's parents, and Mrs Dulwich agreed, wanted as few people as possible to know. Heather was sworn to silence, and Maggie's other friends were told nothing.

Fortunately, it was a cold autumn, and with the help of a baggy jumper, Maggie's condition was kept secret quite easily. It was clear she would be able to complete the first term of her A-Level course, but would not be able to return to school in January.

After Christmas was over, Maggie's parents decided it would be best if she went and stayed somewhere else until the baby was born. Friends might drop in unannounced if she stayed at home, and it would be difficult for her to go out in case she was seen.

Maggie's paternal grandmother lived in Cornwall, alone, since her husband's death five years before and was happy for Maggie to come and stay. At seventy three, Ellen Hanson was an independent, liberal-minded woman who had taken the news of Maggie's pregnancy in her stride. She had been a lecturer in English Literature at Exeter University before she retired in 1966, and was very keen that Maggie should have the chance to continue her A-Level course without too much disruption. Neither she nor Maggie's parents had mentioned what would happen after the baby was born, and Maggie hadn't dared to ask. If she allowed herself to think for too long about what she and Mark had done so carelessly on that warm, summer's night, a terrible heaviness would fall over her, a thick blanket of pain and regret, determined to suffocate her.

On January 2nd 1974, without announcement or fuss,

Maggie's father drove her down to her grandmother's house in Cornwall. Maggie had offered to go on the train, but her father wouldn't hear of it.

'I never expected to have to do this, but you are my daughter. I must see you safely there.'

It would be over six months before she saw her home again and when she did everything would have changed.

She didn't want the baby adopted, but it happened anyway. Her parents weren't prepared to help her bring the child up, and she couldn't manage on her own. They kept all knowledge of the birth from Mark, and because of the enforced secrecy, his relationship with Maggie gradually petered out, as their letters became more and more infrequent. He did try to ring her once when he returned home for the Christmas holiday, but her father answered the phone, and put him off.

During her time in Cornwall, Maggie felt so remote from her previous life that her friendship with Mark soon seemed no more than a dream, achingly poignant, but not real.

In September 1974 she returned to school for her final year. She was an object of gossip and speculation for a few weeks, but with nothing to feed on, it soon died away. Maggie never recovered, not completely. The loss of a child is an emptiness which can never be filled, and only when she accepted that, was she able to move on.

II. David

Mamma frightens me. Sometimes. Nonna says she needs looking after and I must help. I do try. Sometimes. Nonna says she's a bit like toy which has gone wrong and doesn't work properly. I don't really know what she means. None of my toys are like Mamma. I want Mamma to be happy. It's my birthday today but she doesn't look very happy. Nonna says we are all going to do something special today. For my birthday. Mamma too. I feel frightened but I mustn't show it. Nonna wants me to be happy. I do try.

It's very hot. Mamma doesn't like the heat. She's always hiding. Sometimes I go and look for her but she doesn't like it. She gets angry. I am not sure if she loves me. Nonna says she does. I'm not sure. I want to go to the lake, ride on the boat but we're not going there. We are going to someone's house. Nonna says it will be fun. I'm not sure. Mamma is coming too. I don't think she likes fun.

We are going for a picnic at this house. Nonna says there will be nice things to eat. She says the lady whose house it is, is making a cake. My tummy feels funny but I'm not going to tell anyone. I wish I was going to the lake.

Mamma is all right when we go. She's happy, I think. I hope she is. I don't want her to be a broken toy. Not today. Today is my day, Nonna says. Nothing is to spoil it. She says I am to be happy. I do try.

The swimming pool is big. I go and look at it. Nobody notices. It's very deep and blue. It frightens me a little but I love it. I'm alone. Mamma is still talking to the grown-up boy. I think she likes him. She doesn't talk to many people. Perhaps he can mend her.

I stand right on the edge of the pool. It's very hot. I feel a bit dizzy. I think I might fall in, but the grown up boy comes and everything is better. I tell him. I want to go in. He says I can, but at the other end. There are steps there, and the water isn't quite so blue. He's kind and helps me take off my clothes. Mamma is watching us but she doesn't come to the pool. I just want the grown up boy. He looks strong. Mama isn't strong.

There are steps. I can splash a lot. I'm not frightened. I shout to Mamma. It's fun. I'm happy. As long as she doesn't come near.

The water is very cold. I am laughing but it is hard to breathe when the grown up boy carries me away from the steps. He tells me his name is Stephen. He wants to know my name. I tell him. I don't think he hears. There is water in my mouth and I can't speak clearly. We both laugh and I am happy.

In the pool I forget about Mamma. I know she is there but I can't see her. She is hiding again. I don't want to find her. I feel safe with Stephen. He is strong and holds me tightly while we laugh and splash.

I'm back on the steps and Stephen has gone. The water feels warmer now but I'm still shivering. My teeth make a funny noise. I can't stop them. I want Stephen to come back. He will see me if I splash. I am jumping as high as I can. The splashes are very big. l can see nothing. There is only water. I wish Stephen would come.

I can see Mamma again. She is going to jump in the pool. I shout to Stephen. I am frightened. The fun has gone and the water is cold. I don't want to cry. It's my birthday. I don't want to cry.

Stephen is back. He puts a towel round me. The sun is hot but I can't stop shaking. My teeth won't stand still. Mamma is here. I am falling. Something pushed me. I can't save my head. It's an egg. It's going to break.

There is something warm on my neck. I can't see what it is. I feel sick. Mamma is hitting Stephen. I want her to stop. Stephen is my friend. He is very strong. He holds her with one hand and pulls me up with the other. My legs feel wobbly. I am trying to stand. Mamma is making a funny noise. It frightens me. She is not hitting Stephen any more. There is just the noise. It frightens me.

Nonna is here. We are leaving the others behind. My head hurts. I want Stephen but he is with Mamma. She won't let him go. I feel sick and my head hurts. Nonna says she will make it better.

When I touch my head there's a big egg there. I didn't break an egg I made one. Nonna is looking after my egg. It hurts when she touches it but I like her touch. It stops me feeling sick. I feel warmer. My teeth are doing what they're told. I want Stephen.

He is in another room with Mamma. I am going to find him. Nonna wants to stop me but I'm too quick. The egg on my head makes me quick. I want Stephen. He knows about the cake. It's my birthday. I want my cake.

There are a lot of people in the room. I run to Stephen. He knows about my cake. Something happens. I make something terrible happen. Stephen is falling away from me and the red stuff is everywhere. Stephen grabs me. I am shouting at him. I can't take my eyes off the red stuff.

The noise begins. Something is hurt. It gets louder and louder. I am looking at Mamma. I am looking at the red stuff. Mamma is hurting. I am hurting. We are both making the noise. It goes on and on.

III. Maria

It was always the crying which woke her. Not her own. Someone else's. It was a low, monotonous, sobbing, which barely paused for breath, and didn't stop until a nurse went in at 7 am to wake the patient for the early checks.

On that first morning, confused and swimmy from heavy sedation, Maria wondered if she was hearing herself, and she touched her face tentatively to check for tears. Dry fingertips reassured her, and she felt her breathing slow into a more comfortable rhythm. The sobbing continued, like an echo of her own pain, and just loud enough to prevent her from dropping back to sleep. Her door had been left open the previous evening for the night nurse to keep an eye on her, so any sounds could easily be coming from further down the corridor rather than next door. Something raw and relentless about such unbroken grief, made her fear any possible contact, even on the other side of a wall, and she pleaded with a passing nurse to close her door, so that the sound would stop. For nearly a week her appeals went unheeded, a cruelty she found hard to forgive, but then one evening after she had received her final medication for the night, the nurse, on leaving, closed the door firmly behind her. For a few minutes the silence possessed its own strangeness, she had become so used to the chatter as nurses swapped shifts, or talked to other patients, but then she felt her taut muscles relax into the quietness, and tears of relief pricked her eyes.

The next morning, however, she woke again to the sound of sobbing. The door was shut, but the sound remained, a little muffled by the closed door, but unmistakeable. There was no doubt now that it was coming from the adjoining room, and every now and then she would stand, ear pressed to the dividing wall, trying to discern any words behind the sobs of her distraught neighbour. She was both frightened and intrigued by the persistence of the grief. She could understand the enduring nature of the pain behind it, she felt it too, but the sheer, physical effort needed for such sustained sobbing baffled her. To listen to it was exhausting; to experience it must be some kind of Hell. At least that is what she thought during her early weeks in the clinic.

Looking back, she found it hard to describe her state of mind in those first few weeks. She seemed trapped in an unfamiliar world, floating free of all previous associations, although her senses were alert to the point of torture. The sharpness of perception, which had characterised moments in the villa and garden, returned with ever greater intensity, like the drag of nails on metal. Her nerves screamed in agony as she registered every detail of her new surroundings, and every day she longed for the moment when she could return to her room, and crawl into bed, pulling sheet and blankets over her head, like some protective shell.

The place itself wasn't unpleasant. Even in her half drugged state, she realised that it was her response to it that was poisoned, and until that poison was drawn, the healing within its walls, and the beauty beyond them, would remain out of reach.

The Eschmann clinic had only been open a year. The buildings were modern and purpose built and well spread out in the extensive grounds, which had once belonged to the big house, now an administration block. The nearest village was a five kilometre drive down a narrow, mountain, road, and from there it was nearly ten kilometres to pick up the main road into Martigny. Ringed by mountains and nestling in a high valley, the clinic seemed both on top of the world and remote from it. Every window framed a picture postcard view, and only a few metres from the buildings, the clean, clear, quietness closed in, broken occasionally by a cow bell, ghostly in its distant echo, bouncing haphazardly from peak to peak.

When Maria was admitted, the clinic was already full, and new applicants were being turned down on a daily basis. Fortunately, Maria's doctor had a connection, through a friend, with one of the psychiatrists who made up the professional board of directors. The clinic was sponsored by an anonymous Swiss banker, with philanthropic instincts, but the day to day running was left to the distinguished group of psychiatrists and therapists who worked there. Compared to many other similar clinics, the fees were very reasonable, and its reputation was growing rapidly as a centre of excellence for nervous disorders which didn't fit neatly into any particular diagnosis. Maria's case was sufficiently serious and urgent to justify the special pleading on her behalf by her doctor, and arrangements were made to accommodate her immediately after her dramatic breakdown at David's party.

It had been a terrible twenty four hours. The screaming wouldn't stop, and the emergency services had to be called. Maria was forcibly restrained and then removed from the Gales' villa, Sally and Bernardo accompanying her to the nearest hospital, on the outskirts of Rome. David, whose screams soon turned to an uncontrollable shaking, refused to be prised away from Stephen, and Jeannie and Richard offered to look after him until Sally and Bernardo could return. Deeply shocked by their daughter's total collapse, Maria's parents had no choice but to abandon their grandson to the care of almost strangers. Years later Sally wondered how she could have done it, but at the time a creeping numbness had seemed to paralyse all natural feelings, except for her desire to find a place where her daughter could be safe. The doctor's suggestion of The Eschmann clinic was therefore seized upon by both Sally and Bernardo with painful gratitude, and Maria was to fly to Switzerland as soon as she was calm enough to travel. Her parents were advised not to accompany her, but to wait until she was settled and responding to treatment. Instead her doctor would go with her to oversee the heavy sedation necessary to make her manageable. Sally's last glimpse of her daughter, silent at last and barely conscious, as she was loaded onto the ambulance which would take her to Rome airport, seemed part of a nightmare from which she would never awake. The mother's ability to protect and comfort her young had been ripped away and she felt only a raw, helpless, pain as the tail lights of the ambulance disappeared into the warm, Italian, night.

In many ways it was the clinic's highly structured regime which enabled Maria to survive those first desperate weeks. As the sedation was steadily reduced she needed to find a prop somewhere else, and she found it in a routine which did away with personal decisions. Directed by others, she drifted through the days, all her energy sucked into the combat with the searing pain her senses brought her. Voices were louder than they should be, faces cartoonish in their distortion, smells so strong they made her stomach heave, as she struggled to eat the food on her plate. The walls of her room and the corridor outside, were luminous in their whiteness, only relieved by carefully placed paintings, their colours like open wounds, throbbing with life. Left to herself she would never have emerged from under the covers, but that wasn't allowed. Every day had its own discipline and momentum, and she was carried along by it, as unresisting as a leaf drifting down a stream.

At 7 am there was a bang on the door, and a voice informed her that she must be up for breakfast in thirty minutes. The voice was never harsh or bullying, but it was firm. It accepted no possibility of refusal. For the first few days a nurse came into her room while she dressed, brushed her teeth and hair, and made her bed. She was told the order in which to do things; no deviation was allowed. Once her actions were natural, unthinking, she was left alone, and it never occurred to her to rebel. Survival lay in conforming and she was quick to learn this first lesson.

Breakfast was more of an ordeal. It was quite a long walk to the restaurant, which was in another block, and the corridors were confusing in their uniform whiteness.

'Like a rat in a maze', she muttered to herself as she retraced her steps for the third time, searching for the exit which led to the path, which led to the block, where the restaurant was. It reminded her of the first day at secondary school, where everybody seemed to know where they were going except for her. For a few minutes, a familiar feeling of panic brought her back to the real world, before she slid away again into the surreal existence which had no anchor yet in the past.

Every morning she had the same for breakfast. There was plenty of choice but decisions took too much energy. She put two croissants and two tiny jars of jam on her plate and asked for a black coffee. The only time she had something different was on a Friday when there were pancakes. Maria was surprised; they seemed so un-European but she enjoyed them. It was a change.

At 8.15 am it was time for her Community group. She was put with the other new admissions, and because the clinic was so full, their group was small. In the first few sessions they were told about the rules and regulations of the clinic; phones, when they were allowed to have them, must only be used for ten minutes at a time, no food was to be brought into their rooms, and under no circumstances was there to be any physical contact with other patients. Everyone in the group accepted what they were told with stupefied resignation. They were all still too heavily sedated to resist. Perhaps they would later, Maria wondered dreamily, as she too nodded in agreement.

Towards the end of the second week, someone new joined the group. A young girl, not more than sixteen years old, was brought in by a nurse, just after the session had begun. She was of slight build, with a thin, pale face, and dark rings under her eyes. There was a hurried consultation between the nurse and the group leader, a young man, who had been introduced to them as a therapist, not a doctor. He seemed reluctant at first to accept the new admission, but the nurse was firm, and he appeared to have no choice.

The girl's name was Lucie, and she was a French speaking Swiss from Martigny.

No other information was given but Philippe, the therapist, hoped the group would make her welcome. There was an empty chair next to Maria and he steered the girl gently towards it. Maria smiled at the newcomer, feeling a sudden pang of compassion for someone who seemed more miserable and frightened than herself. There was barely a flicker of response from Lucie, however, who caught Maria's eye for just a moment, before turning away to take her seat. She made no contribution to the session, which finished at 10 o'clock, and as soon as they were free to go, she hurried away, eyes down, shoulders hunched, and without a backward glance.

The next morning she turned up on time but was no more forthcoming. During the session they were all encouraged to talk, to interact, the main purpose of the group. Philippe tried gently, in fact quite skilfully, Maria had to admit, to tease out any overnight anxieties and fears. He very quickly created an atmosphere which was calm and reassuring, so that most members of the group felt happy to contribute. It was soon clear to Maria that nearly all of them were there for depression, including a few for suicide attempts. The group consisted entirely of men, except for herself and Lucie, although in the clinic as a whole the numbers seemed to be fairly equal. At every session, two seats were always left free, so that she and Lucie could sit together, and although she never said anything, Maria could sense Lucie was grateful for the gesture.

Throughout the rest of the day Maria saw nothing more of Lucie. She had her own carefully controlled schedule to follow, and there was little opportunity to investigate where the girl might have got to. Maria assumed she would have her own tight programme, their only overlap being the daily Community group.

At 10.15 am, three days a week, Maria met with her psychiatrist, Dr Williams. He was another relatively young man, like the therapist, and always looked concerned. At each meeting he ran through the usual routine of questions. How is your mood? Do you feel like hurting yourself? How are you sleeping? Do you have nightmares?

To begin with, she thought very carefully about her answers, anxious to create the right impression, but after a time she became bored with the repetition and answered more spontaneously, almost without thinking at all. Dr Williams seemed pleased when she reached this stage, and began to vary the questions from meeting to meeting, so that she had to think again, but the spontaneity remained.

Following this one to one session, the morning finished with a process group with her social worker. It was with a different set of people from the Community group, all women this time, although there was still no sign of Lucie. A lot of work was done in this group to help the patients combat negative thoughts. A favourite exercise was to ask each member of the group to write down a negative thought, and then three positive ones to counteract it. Several women cried when they were asked to read theirs out, and one launched into a rant on the importance of exercise until the social worker, Michelle, politely cut her off. Maria soon became aware that all her negative thoughts were connected with David, and it frightened her. She didn't find it easy to produce positive thoughts to set against them, and became increasingly resentful at Michelle's insistence that she should try.

Lunch came as a welcome break, and gave time for her jangled nerves to settle, before she embarked on the afternoon programme. On the whole, this was the more relaxed part of the day, divided into two parts; an education group followed by what was loosely termed recreational therapy. The latter was the only session where there was a certain amount of free choice, which at first Maria found difficult to cope with. Making decisions required an awareness of her situation, which was upsetting and caused a feeling of panic, familiar and yet terrifying. During the first few weeks she simply refused to make a choice, and retreated to her room, hiding under the covers in confused misery, until she was fetched by a nurse and allocated an activity. The whole process was humiliating, and the worst part of her strange and taxing days.

It was on one of these occasions when she had retreated to her room, praying that this time her disappearance would not be noticed too quickly, that she heard the sobbing again. For the past week she had woken to silence, unexpected and disconcerting in its strangeness, as the sobbing had become almost a comfort in its predictability. Now the sobbing was there again, in the middle of the afternoon, as persistent and haunting as ever. This time Maria could not contain her curiosity. She had to find out who it was.

She opened her door cautiously, and glanced quickly down the long, white, corridor. It was empty, as she would expect at that time of day, with every patient involved in a chosen activity. There was also no sign of a nurse sent to drag her back to such an activity ; perhaps at last they were going to leave her alone. Closing her own door behind her, she stood completely still for a moment, holding her breath, as she made sure the sobbing really was coming from the next door room. Convinced, she moved towards it and raised a hand to knock. For a split second she hesitated, surprised by her own boldness, and in that split second, she was also certain that she already knew the answer to her question.

She had to knock several times, her neighbour obviously deafened by her own unremitting sobbing. She knew the sobber was female as the corridors were segregated on the basis of gender. In any case no man would sob like that, with such determination and endurance.

At last she was heard, and the sobbing stopped. The silence was unnerving, both inside and outside the room, and Maria had to break it.

'Hello. It's Maria. Can I help?'

Seconds passed, so slowly, as if time itself was grinding

to a halt. And then there was the barely perceptible sound of movement, the knob turned, and the door was left ajar. It wasn't much of a welcome, but it was enough.

She pushed the door open further with her foot, until she had a clear view of the hunched figure, sitting on the side of the bed. Still she hesitated, before slipping into the room. It seemed like an invasion somehow. Then her name, spoken in hardly more than a whisper, reassured her and she stepped inside, closing the door firmly behind her, with a slight movement backwards.

There was a long silence as they stared at each other, uncertain of the next step, and aware of each other's fragility.

'It is you', Maria breathed, as if to raise her voice would be too intrusive.

The girl nodded and lowered her eyes. Her arms were rigid with tension, and she was gripping the bed cover so tightly with both hands, that her knuckles had turned white with the strain. The sobbing had stopped but she was breathing heavily, as if exhausted by some huge, physical effort.

For the first time since she arrived at the clinic, Maria realised she was in the presence of a pain, far greater than her own. The girl needed help, and she was the only person, at that moment, who could give it.

Moving towards the bed, she put a hand on the girl's shoulder, willing her to calm down. At Maria's touch the tears started again, but they were different now. They rolled down her cheeks silently, as if they alone were proof enough of the agony inside, and there was no need to sob.

Noticing a box of tissues on a small table next to the bed, Maria reached over and took one to hand to Lucie.

'Do you want to talk?' She said gently as the girl wiped her face hurriedly, obviously ashamed of such a display of uncontrollable emotion.

'I don't know. Not today. Sometimes perhaps. No one can help. It's no good.'

She spoke quietly but quickly to prevent interruption, glancing briefly at Maria to see her reaction.

Maria smiled for the first time in weeks.

'That's okay. Whenever you like. I'm only next door after all.'

Lucie didn't smile but instead looked steadily at Maria, her eyes full of puzzled enquiry.

Maria immediately sensed the girl's need for further reassurance, and rubbed her shoulder firmly to support her words. Now, with a hint of a smile, Lucie grabbed Maria's hand, and spoke more strongly.

'Come again soon, Maria. Please. So we can talk.'

Maria nodded and turned to go. She felt stronger too.

Outside, in the corridor, there was the sound of rapid footsteps and someone knocking impatiently on a door. They had come to find her. There was no escape.

Maria was reprimanded quite severely for her visit to Lucie's room. Contact between patients was strictly controlled, particularly when it was unsupervised.

This rule, or convention, was explained to patients as soon as they arrived at the clinic, although in Maria's eyes no very sound reasons were given to justify its importance. It was the staff nurse who oversaw the corridor who spoke to her, and warned that the breach would have to be reported to Dr Williams. Maria was glad when she heard this, as she intended to raise it with him anyway at their next session. She felt different after the visit to Lucie's room, more decisive, more in control. Something had changed, and it felt like an improvement.

Dr Williams was sympathetic. He listened carefully to what she had to say, and made no attempt to ask the usual questions. It was if they had moved onto a different level of communication altogether. Unlike the staff nurse, Dr Williams didn't seem at all angry or disturbed by Maria's transgression, but rather pleased, even excited.

'Do you think you can help this young woman?' he said thoughtfully when Maria had finished relating exactly what was said and done.

'I'm not sure but I should like to try,' she replied eagerly. 'We are the only two women in our Community group, so there is a connection there already.'

'That's true'. Dr Williams spoke slowly, tapping his desk top with his pencil. 'It could work, but it won't be easy. Lucie is a very unhappy young woman who isn't responding to our usual treatment. Are you prepared for that? It could be a very upsetting experience for you.'

Dr Williams' gaze sharpened as he looked intently at Maria.

'You would be putting yourself at risk,' he added quietly. 'You are vulnerable too, you know.'

'Yes, I know. But that could be an advantage. Surely it's worth a go?'

There was a long pause before the doctor spoke again and when he did it was to ask what seemed to be a totally unrelated question.

'Have you had any visitors yet, Maria?'

She shook her head.

'Well I think it's time you did. Leave it to me. In the meantime your recreational therapy is to talk to Lucie. I suggest a walk up the mountain might be a good start for both of you. We can suggest some paths to take.'

The pattern was set and on the whole it worked. They took the path up the mountain on many occasions, and they never tired of it. There were setbacks, of course, that was to be expected and she had been warned. One came very early, and it threatened to ruin everything.

One afternoon, following her consultation with Dr Williams, Maria went to knock on Lucie's door again. It was the beginning of the activity period, and for once she was keen to get involved. Lucie had refused to co- operate and attend any session, except for the Community group where she was with Maria, with the result that she spent most of her time alone in her room, while Dr Williams and the rest of the board tried to put together a treatment programme which would work. Maria's recruitment to this plan was unorthodox, but Dr Williams had spoken so persuasively at the patients' board, that his colleagues had decided to support the idea on a temporary and experimental basis.

Maria was pleased but nervous. She wanted so much to help and she didn't want to let Dr Williams down. With each session, her trust in the young psychiatrist was growing, and their conversations were becoming more relaxed and intimate. Prompted by the insights she had gained in the process group she now talked more freely of her difficult relationship with David. She wasn't yet completely honest about her feelings, but it now seemed possible that moment might come, and with that thought the weight on her heart had begun to lift.

She knocked three times quite loudly, but there was no reply. As far as she knew there had been no sobbing since her last visit. She had heard two of the nurses discussing this change one morning when she was tidying her room, and she hoped it might have something to do with her earlier visit. The sobbing had been distressing, but the silence was equally disconcerting, in a different sort of way.

She knocked again, even more loudly, pressing her ear to the door, to see if she could detect any sound of movement. There was none. Rising panic made her mouth go dry and she struggled to control her feelings. She knew she mustn't break down. Lucie might need her. If something had happened, it was important she kept calm.

At the far end of the corridor a figure appeared. Help was at hand. Maria waved but didn't shout, her mouth was too dry. The figure was running now, but still seemed to be coming so slowly.

'I can't get a reply. I think something may be wrong.'

Maria was surprised at how calm she sounded, when her heart was beating so frantically in her chest.

The nurse knocked on the door, calling Lucie's name in a firm, loud, voice.

'Can you open the door Lucie. It's Nurse Gilbert. We need to talk to you.'

While she was speaking she turned the door knob, pushing against the door as she did so.

'It's stuck,' she said to Maria, 'or it's been wedged shut. Either way we can't get in. Can you wait here while I go to the nurses' station and call for help.'

Maria nodded. 'Yes, of course. But please hurry, I'm frightened.'

Nurse Gilbert gave her a quick look and then patted her arm.

'You're doing very well. I'll be back in a moment.'

Alone again, outside the door, Maria prayed. Despite her strict catholic upbringing, she didn't really believe in prayer, but there seemed nothing else she could do. 'Let her be all right. Please God. Let her be alright.'

What happened next remained confused and upsetting in her mind for a long time, but through it all, she remained calm and in control of her own feelings, and she was proud of that.

The door had to be broken down as Lucie had barricaded it so effectively. Dr Williams and the staff nurse were first into the room after the door had been opened, pushing their way past piled up furniture, to get to Lucie, sprawled on the bed, unmoving and deathly pale. There was blood everywhere, soaking into the bedclothes and splattered across the walls, like some experiment in modern art.

Maria, forgotten by everyone in the rush to save Lucie, couldn't see very clearly what happened next. Pressed against the far wall of the corridor, she watched as a stretcher bed was wheeled in, and Lucie was hooked up to oxygen and some sort of drip. She was then wheeled away, Dr Williams and the staff nurse walking quickly to keep up with the stretcher, and the white, gleaming corridor rapidly emptied again, like some huge, efficient, drain.

Maria slid to the floor, her legs buckling under her from the nervous strain. There was no- one to see her and she was glad of that. Lucie was still alive, and she had kept her head. There was a lot to be thankful for.

The setback—Maria never heard it called by its rightful name—delayed the walks up the mountain but it didn't stop them. For several weeks, Lucie was under intense medical supervision, and Maria was only allowed to see her very occasionally. Dr Williams fought hard to keep the original plan in place, as one or two of the board were anxious to remove Lucie to another clinic altogether, where she could receive treatment more appropriate to her condition. Dr Williams disagreed strongly. He still believed in Maria's influence, and he wanted his idea to have a chance. Fortunately, most of the board continued to back him, if a little reluctantly, and the plan remained on course.

It was at the end of the first week, after Lucie's breakdown, when Maria received her first visitors. It was six months since she had seen her parents, although she had spoken to them both on the phone, once a week, since her treatment began. There had been no contact at all with friends, but then she didn't have many, and certainly no-one she would want to call regularly. Once or twice, she felt an intense longing to see Stephen, but she quickly suppressed the feeling as ridiculous and unfeasible. After all she hardly knew him. Thoughts of David haunted her all the time, but she didn't want to see or speak to him. She felt guilty and ashamed of such unnatural feelings, but she couldn't shift them. Just as David's screams had merged with hers, on that terrible summer's day, so too had their pain. She carried it for both of them, and that was as much as she could bear.

Dr Williams had been as good as his word. Straight after the session, when the subject had been raised, he had contacted Maria's parents and suggested the time had come when a visit would be appropriate, even helpful perhaps.

'Maria is making steady progress, and there has been a development in her treatment, which we are very hopeful about,' he said to Sally on the phone. 'I think a visit from you now will help to reassure her that a return to normal life is a real possibility, and maybe sooner than she thinks. Please. Come as soon as you can.'

Sally and Bernardo were delighted, of course, at such good news, but also a little anxious. If they were honest, life had been so much easier since Maria had been in the clinic, and the thought of her return threw everything into turmoil again. To begin with, David had been deeply upset, even traumatised by his mother's behaviour, but since early December he had seemed more settled, as if at last, he was coming to terms with what had happened, or just beginning to forget about it. Bernardo favoured the latter, but Sally wasn't so sure. She was convinced that such extreme events would have a long term effect on the boy, particularly if he was burying feelings he couldn't yet deal with. To have his mother return too soon, still vulnerable and fragile, might be the worst possible situation for David, and Sally feared for his happiness and stability. They decided not to tell him they were going to visit his mother. Instead a story was concocted about meeting up with old friends for a few days which the boy seemed to accept quite happily. Since Maria's departure to the clinic an au pair, Gina, had been employed to help look after David and assist Sally with light chores. She was a cheerful, uncomplicated, girl, whose laughter and high spirits made them all feel better. David took to her immediately, and the two of them were soon inseparable.

Sally even began to feel a little jealous, as their laughter and voices filled the villa, but she only had to glance at her grandson's face, smiling and relaxed, to regret her pettiness. Gina gave David the chance to be a child again, carefree, and living for the moment, and without the apprehension and uncertainty which had made his relationship with his mother, so difficult, even frightening. Being told that Gina would be in sole charge of him for several days made the boy's face light up with pleasure, and so all was set for the visit to go ahead.

Sally and Bernardo flew from Rome to Geneva, and then hired a car to drive through France to Martigny, and then on to the clinic. Speaking to Maria on the phone, the day before they left, Sally was surprised by something different in her daughter's voice. It had a firmer, lighter tone than usual, as if she had at last seized back some sort of control of her thoughts and feelings. Sally felt her spirits lift a little. She hoped it was a good sign.

They arrived at the clinic after lunch on the last Friday in January. The journey from Martigny had been slow, as recent falls of heavy snow were still being cleared from the narrow, mountain road, but the weather was steadily improving, and by the time they reached the clinic, blue skies and sparkling snow made it appear the perfect refuge. Dr Williams met them in reception and took them to his office.

'I wanted a word before you saw Maria. As I said on the phone, she is making good progress, and although there is still a way to go, we are hopeful. There is also something else I need to mention, just in case it comes up in conversation with your daughter. I know it may sound a bit unorthodox but she is helping us with another patient, a young girl, Lucie, whom she's befriended and who seems to trust her.

She's in recovery at the moment from a suicide attempt, and Maria is visiting occasionally. When Lucie is more stable, the plan is for them to spend more time together, go for walks, talk to each other. It's not without risk, of course, I'm sure you understand that, but we think it's worth a try. It could help both of them quite significantly or,' he hesitated, 'it could go disastrously wrong and set them both back. We don't usually encourage close, personal, bonds but in this case we think it might work. They are both intelligent, sensitive, young women, and when you are dealing with the mind, there are sometimes places a doctor can never reach, and only a friend can.

I very much hope you will be happy to support us in this experiment.'

Sally, listening intently, winced a little at the word experiment, and glanced at Bernardo. He seemed lost in thought or had switched off completely from the whole business. Sally knew how difficult her husband found it to cope with Maria's psychological problems, and that he felt guilty about the part he thought he had played in causing them. She had tried many times to persuade him that he wasn't responsible, but she could tell he wasn't convinced. She also knew he wouldn't want to engage with the doctor and his ideas, and it would be up to her to do that. Sometimes she felt lonely, even resentful, of the way he abandoned Maria's problems to her, but she had to accept it. If their daughter was to recover, it would probably be an uncomfortable and frustrating road, but they had no choice, she was sure of that. They could only hope and trust.

Taking a deep breath, Sally smiled brightly at Dr Williams.

'Thank you for being so frank, we appreciate it. If you think this is the best way forward, of course we are happy to go along with it.'

Dr Williams appeared visibly relieved at her reply, although he looked enquiringly at Bernardo, who had remained stubbornly silent.

'And does that go for you too sir', he said after a slight pause.

'Yes, yes of course,' Bernardo said quietly. 'We are in your hands doctor.'

Something had changed. Sally felt it immediately, as they entered the visitors' lounge, and Maria came across the room to greet them. The strained look had gone from her eyes, and there was a smile on her face.

They all hugged without words, and when Maria stepped back a little, Sally could see tears shining in her eyes.

'Thanks for coming,' Maria said, her voice rough with emotion. 'How are you both?'

'We're fine. What about you?' Sally said quickly. 'Dr Williams seems to think you're making good progress.'

'Oh! You've spoken to him already. I didn't know that.'

Maria seemed a little put out, and the smile disappeared.

' He asked to see us. We couldn't refuse,' Sally said calmly.

'What else did he say? Was that it?'

Something of the old resentment, even coldness, had returned to Maria's voice, and Sally felt her heart sink.

'No, not quite. He wanted to tell us a bit about Lucie and how he thinks you can help her. He seems very keen on the idea, and obviously thinks it might help you too.'

The colour drained from Maria's cheeks, and she bit her lip in an effort to contain her anger.

'He shouldn't have done that. The–' she hesitated slightly, 'thing with Lucie is between him and me. It's nothing to do with you.'

'I think Dr Williams sees it as part of your therapy,' Sally replied quietly, 'and he thought we should know about it. There's no need to get upset.'

Sally felt herself trembling slightly, and she clutched the back of a nearby chair, to steady herself.

'Let's sit down,' Bernardo said suddenly, moving towards a group of easy chairs near the window.

Sally followed him but Maria didn't move, and glancing back Sally saw tears running down her daughter's face, which she made no attempt to check. Shaken, and uncertain what to do next, Sally sat down, and it was left to Bernardo to rescue Maria.

For some minutes all three sat in silence, their pain strangely at odds with the beauty beyond the glass. The low afternoon sun still caught the tops of the surrounding peaks, which were glowing like white sentinels against the blue sky, as they gazed down at the lengthening shadows below. Just beyond the window, the path winding between the banks of piled snow, was well swept but empty. The whole scene was one of silent stillness, its beauty held suspended in a timeless moment.

Maria didn't weep for long. Sally was right, she had changed. She found it easier now to control her feelings when they threatened to overwhelm her, and with a shy laugh, she dried her eyes and smiled again at her parents.

'Sorry,' she said quietly. 'I shouldn't have reacted like that.'

Sally looked up at the new gentleness in Maria's voice, and Bernardo leaned across and patted his daughter on the shoulder. A semblance of peace had been restored, although during the rest of the visit, a certain awkwardness still remained, which prevented any real closeness.

Leaving to drive back to Martigny and their hotel, they decided not to return for another visit the following day, even though they were booked in for one. Maria had expressed no desire to see any more of them, although she knew it was possible, and they felt the need to respect her unspoken wish. In a way, it was a great relief. There had been progress, they could both see that, but Maria wasn't ready for them yet. All her energy was needed for her recovery, and they weren't part of that. It lay in the hands of strangers to complete the healing, and in the sadness of that thought, Sally's heart turned gratefully towards the south again, and the boy they had left behind.

The path was taking them to a village half way up the mountain. It was the highest settlement in the surrounding area, and only able to be reached on foot during the heaviest snowfalls. There was a road, but it was too steep and dangerous for ordinary vehicles, when it was half a metre deep in snow and ice. The path, however, had been made by local farmers, so they could bring extra winter feed to their cattle, which roamed freely over the lower slopes of the mountain, and was well maintained. Trouble had been taken to find the easiest route for walking, but even so, some stretches required basic mountaineering skills, which were indicated on the map by thick, red lines either side of the dotted line which marked the path. The map was produced locally, and regularly updated to take account of changes to well-known paths, or the introduction of new ones.

The walk was, therefore, quite an adventure, but they were well prepared. Dr Williams had insisted they both attend some sessions in mountain awareness, which included an introduction to the skills needed for serious Alpine walking. The sessions were led by a local guide, Adrien, and were popular with visitors to the area, who didn't want to ski or snowboard, but still wanted to explore the higher slopes of the mountain.

The bond between the two young women had strengthened considerably during the weeks since Lucie's suicide attempt. There had been some dark times when Lucie had refused to see or speak to anyone, but Maria hadn't been discouraged. She felt instinctively that the younger girl needed her, and she refused to be rebuffed. The visits were arranged by Dr Williams, who was monitoring Lucie's mental state very closely. After the suicide attempt, she had been moved to a special observation room, where nurses were able to keep a twenty four hour watch on her. There had been a heavy loss of blood from her botched attempt to cut her wrists, but the physical injuries soon began to heal. The ones in her head would take a lot longer.

With every visit, whatever Lucie's reaction, Maria felt her own confidence growing, as she gradually rediscovered an inner strength, she thought she had lost for ever. Her life now had a sense of purpose, and each morning she woke, eager and excited, to make a start on the day. There was always the chance that she might be able to see Lucie, or if not, she could discuss how things were going with Dr Williams. He had increased his scheduled meetings with her since she had begun to help Lucie, and most weeks she saw him every day. If he was very busy, the meeting would be very brief, but he always tried to find the time to see her at some point in the day.

Maria knew that all the time and attention she was being given wasn't just to do with Lucie. It was as much to do with her, her therapy, as it was with Lucie. In the past she would have regarded such treatment as condescending, even manipulative, but now her enthusiasm for the task of helping another had banished all that. Somehow, it didn't matter any more to her why things were being done, it was what was done which was important. For the first time, someone else's sufferings were more important than her own; a strange lifeline, but one she clung to with desperate hope.

They had started early, as soon as it was light. It would take them most of the day to reach the village, where they were booked into a small hotel for the night. The plan was to return the next day as long as the weather was good, and if not, they could stay on for a bit longer. The proprietor was a friend of Dr Williams and understood a little of the girls' circumstances. He was in support of his friend's 'walk and talk' therapy, and happy to keep a discreet eye on any patients sent his way.

Two days before they set out, there had been a very heavy fall of snow, but the local farmers had quickly got to work, and the path was passable again. Adrien had gone over the route very thoroughly with them both, highlighting the dangerous stretches, where if they stepped off the path, they could find themselves up to their necks, or worse, in deep snowdrifts.

'If by any chance the weather turns nasty you must stop and wait for the storm to pass,' he had said the night before they set out. 'At the moment the forecast is quite good, but things can change very rapidly in the mountains. You must be prepared.'

Maria felt a shiver of excitement at this hint of danger, followed by a strong, protective feeling towards her younger companion.

'We'll be sensible,' she said, smiling at Adrien. 'You have taught us well.'

The first few kilometres were easy walking, across the flat floor of the high mountain valley, which contained the clinic and a few scattered farms, and they made good time. Maria was by far the stronger physically, and had to adjust her natural pace a little, so that Lucie could keep up with her. Where the path required single file, it seemed natural for her to take the lead, and Lucie seemed content to follow, quite literally, in her footsteps. They were both carrying rucksacks, containing basic emergency equipment, as well as a packed lunch, although Maria had insisted that extra water, spare batteries and the two, lightweight, sleeping bags should go into her rucksack, to reduce Lucie's load a little.

Dr Williams was delighted with the confident and organised manner in which Maria approached the whole expedition. The experimental therapy certainly seemed to be working for Maria; he wasn't so sure about Lucie. The younger girl obviously trusted Maria and was happy in her company, but she hadn't yet opened up to her friend as completely as Dr Williams had hoped. Some barrier was still to be overcome, and so far there was no sign of that happening. Time away from the clinic might be just the catalyst needed to bring it about, Dr Williams said to himself, to stifle any professional doubts he was having about the progress of his experiment. He knew it was quite a high risk strategy, but he was determined to continue with it.

Whenever the path allowed them to walk abreast, Maria and Lucie fell easily into a relaxed and familiar pattern of conversation. Lucie asked lots of questions and Maria did her best to answer them. To begin with, they were practical questions about the day ahead, as if Lucie needed to reassure herself constantly that Maria was in charge, and knew what she was doing. Then, after a while, they became more personal, focusing on Maria's life in Italy, her family, and what had brought her to the clinic.

At first, Maria had found such questioning difficult to deal with, but once she realised Lucie wasn't just being nosey, but found comfort in these strange, one sided, conversations, she was happy to go along with it. Some questions she avoided answering, particularly those to do with David, and she would quickly deflect the conversation on to another topic. If Lucie noticed these refusals, she didn't comment on them.

They made good progress on the level ground, walking briskly to keep warm, their mountain boots gripping the icy surface of the packed down snow, with pleasing efficiency. The sun was slow to appear above the nearby peaks, but when it did the brilliance of the lower slopes dazzled their eyes, and they stopped for a few minutes to find their sunglasses, and check the map. In the crisp cold of the mountain air, the sun posed no threat to Maria, and she felt her old fear of its scorching power slipping away. She no longer sought the shade like some timid, nocturnal, creature, but revelled in the bright, clear, light which gave such sharp definition to shape and colour. The sky was a deep blue, with just a few white, fluffy clouds gathering slowly in the west, and they both felt in high spirits as they turned their backs on the valley and began the gradual ascent towards the village above. The gradient wasn't very steep and for a while they could keep up their previous pace, although stopping now and then to gaze back across the valley towards the clinic, to measure how far they had come.

Before long the path disappeared into a thick band of fir

trees, which girdled the lower slopes, like a pelmet, and the valley was lost to view. Among the trees, the quiet closed in on them, and they automatically lowered their voices, whispering to each other with a barely suppressed excitement, as they emerged into yet another clearing in the trees. Ringed with fir trees, laden with snow, they seemed like magical places, untouched by man. The path rarely crossed the clearing, but rather skirted its edge, as if unwilling to disturb such perfect whiteness. After each new fall of snow even the tracks of small animals were erased, as if nature herself wanted to start afresh, again and again. The untouched beauty of the snow was tempting, but Maria and Lucie knew better than to leave the path, even for a moment, as such beauty could be deadly.

There was no way of knowing how deep the drifts of snow were, and without skis or snow shoes, they could easily swallow you whole. Adrien had impressed this fact on them more than once, giving an example of a walker who was assumed to have done just that, and who disappeared into the snow for years. His body was found eventually when the snow retreated much further than usual during a particularly warm summer, and he was discovered lying only a few metres from the path.

'One slip and the mountain will grab you,' Adrien had warned, anxious to instil a healthy fear of possible hazards in both young women. 'Like the sea, a mountain is a great force of nature and needs to be respected. If you remember that, you should survive okay,' he concluded with a smile, anxious not to undermine their confidence too much as that too could be dangerous.

Emerging from the belt of trees towards midday, they became aware of how thick the bank of clouds had become towards the west. There was still some blue sky but it was disappearing fast. Away from the shelter of the trees, a stiff breeze whipped the snow against their faces, and they hurried to pull up their hoods and wind their scarves round the lower half of their faces.

'I don't think this was forecast,' Maria said anxiously, as fresh snow, blown by the wind, settled on the path ahead. 'We'd better get a move on before the path gets wiped out'.

Despite the wind and snow, they increased their pace as much as they could, keeping an eye on the wooden posts, which were placed at intervals along the path, to mark its zigzag course across the tracts of snow which formed the upper slopes of the mountain.

They walked in single file so that they could keep to the middle of the path, and after half an hour of fairly brisk walking, Maria, who was leading, became aware that Lucie had dropped quite a long way behind, and was obviously struggling against the rising wind. She waited for the girl to catch up, and as she did so, the last tiny patch of blue sky was blotted out by the heavy bank of clouds, dark and threatening, which was racing towards them from the west. Powdery snow stirred up by the wind merged with large, swirling, snowflakes descending from the leaden sky, and for a moment Maria lost sight of Lucie through the driving snow, as the girl battled her way towards her. Adrien had warned them of sudden changes in the weather on the mountain, but she hadn't expected anything quite so dramatic, or so rapid.

'In the event of a sudden snowstorm seek shelter immediately and wait for it to clear.'

Maria remembered the advice with frightening clarity, and she knew they must act on it at once. Lucie was trembling with exertion and fear when she reached Maria, and it was obvious she was looking to the older woman to make a decision about what to do next.

'We must keep moving until we find some suitable shelter,' Maria said calmly, 'the sooner the better, so keep your eyes open for anything which might do.'

Lucie nodded but said nothing.

After resting for a few minutes, her face had become pale and pinched with the cold, and Maria had a sudden misgiving about the girl's ability to cope physically with the worsening conditions.

'Let's get on,' she shouted as cheerfully as she could above the wind, 'and look out for the posts. Whatever we do, we must stick to the path.'

Over the next hour the conditions became steadily more difficult, as they struggled from post to post, fearful of losing the path altogether in the blizzard. The wind was so strong they found it hard to raise their heads, although they had long since swapped sunglasses for goggles.

Every now and then, Maria stopped to allow Lucie to catch up. If she fell only a few metres behind she disappeared into the blizzard, and Maria's greatest fear was that they might lose each other, and stumble away from the path in their panic.

'You must try to keep up with me,' she mouthed at Lucie. 'Hang on to my rucksack if you like and I'll slow down a bit.'

Lucie nodded and tried hard to smile, but Maria could see that she was totally exhausted. She wouldn't be able to keep going much longer; they had to find some shelter and quickly. Peering through the swirling snow until her eyes ached with the strain, Maria looked desperately for anything which might provide them with even the minimum of shelter. Adrien had told them that there were small huts along the route, constructed by farmers to store food for cattle during the summer months, and they were often quite near to the path. If they could find one of those, they could sit the storm out in reasonable safety. If not, they would just have to improvise some sort of camp on the path itself, and hope for the best. Maria knew she ought to put these two possibilities to Lucie, but something held her back. It was clear the younger girl needed all her energy just to keep going, and was relying on Maria to cope with everything else.

It was just before two o'clock when Maria suddenly spotted a dark shape, coming and going, through the curtain of snow, blown viciously, to and fro, by the gusting wind. For a few minutes she thought her eyes were playing tricks, a mirage of shelter in the terrible whiteness, but when the shape persisted, and even became clearer as they struggled forward, her heart leapt with hope.

It was a small hut, some ten metres from the path, and already half buried in the drifting snow. Two rows of posts, a couple of metres apart, indicated the likelihood of a safe path, although it was much more deeply covered in snow than the path they were on. Nevertheless, they would have to risk it. To get in the dry and out of the biting wind were becoming essential; there was no time for hesitation.

Turning to shout instructions, Maria was shocked by the look of numb misery in Lucie's eyes. Indicating the hut and the barely discernible path which led up to it, she grabbed the girl's hand and stepped off the main path. Immediately, she sank up to her waist in the soft snow, before her feet struck something firmer. Struggling forward, dragging Lucie behind her, she ploughed her way towards the hut. When they got nearer to it the snow wasn't quite so deep, and although there was a padlock on the door it wasn't locked. It was hard work easing the door open, but they managed it eventually, Lucie helping as well, revived a little by the thought of shelter at last.

Inside, they were both pleasantly surprised by what they found. On one side of the hut bales of straw were piled up to the roof, but the rest of it had been made into quite a comfortable den. Blankets had been thrown over straw bales, carefully arranged to form a long seat or couch, next to which was a small, wooden table. Under the window, now almost completely blocked by snow, were two rough shelves, home to a number of useful items. A large torch, a small primus stove, two mugs, and canisters containing tea, coffee and several unopened packets of biscuits were lined up neatly on the top shelf, while underneath there was a pack of six large bottles of water, a small first aid kit, a Swiss Army knife, a length of neatly coiled rope and more paraffin for the primus stove.

'All mod cons here I see,' Maria said cheerfully as they pulled the door to behind them. 'I think we're going to be all right now.'

And they were—all right, if that is how best to describe what happened next. It is tempting to use more superlatives but all right will do. Cut off from the world, threatened by the elements, and with no other distraction, they only had each other to turn to. And so that is what they did. Having eaten their packed lunch, and made a hot drink, they began to talk. It seemed the inevitable, even the right thing to do, and neither of them questioned such a natural impulse.

Colour gradually came back into Lucie's cheeks as the questions began, and this time there were no refusals. At last Maria found herself able to talk about David, not with ease, the pain was still there, but with a frankness, which surprised even herself. Lucie seemed to sense that something had freed itself up in Maria's head, and she questioned and listened with quiet sympathy.

Maria had spoken briefly, on previous occasions, of her time in Durham and her meeting with Matthew but nothing about the pregnancy and how everything had eventually fallen apart.

Now, with the unerring instinct of someone picking at a scab, Lucie returned to those gaps in the story which Maria had been so reluctant to fill in, and slowly but persistently, drew out the truth.

It was a passionate affair from the start, the student love between Maria and Matthew, and it took over their lives completely. Obsessed with each other, they lived only for the moment, neglecting their work and with no thought for the future. It was an unreal, selfish and dreamlike life which only came to an end when late in their second year, Maria became pregnant. Initially, they were both excited at the news and, in those very early days, they even discussed names; David if it was a boy, Emma if a girl.

Then six weeks after the pregnancy had been confirmed by a doctor at the university health centre, reality caught up with Maria, and she changed her mind. She didn't want a baby, she wasn't ready to be a mother, she was too young. In a panic, she begged Matthew to help her to arrange an abortion, but he refused, horrified by the suggestion. Time slipped away as they fought each other over the fate of their unborn child, but they did nothing. Maria was too afraid to act alone, and Matthew refused to give in.

When the two sets of parents were told of the pregnancy things became even more complicated. Maria's parents insisted on marriage, and even though Matthew knew his relationship with Maria was already over, he was too weak to resist. After the marriage, Maria, frightened and angry, at being forced to bear a child she didn't want, refused to have any more to do with Matthew. Their love died as quickly and violently as it had arisen and they were both left bewildered and suffering. From the moment he was born, Maria found it hard to look at the baby, let alone love him.

She called him David, as they had agreed, although more out of indifference than anything else. Resentment at the situation she had been forced into gradually turned into a chilling, corroding, bitterness, which left her cold and dead inside. Diagnosed with severe post- natal depression, she lived in a state of black misery for weeks and months after the birth, until her doctor, convinced that her post-natal depression had become something even more serious and permanent, recommended a change of scene. Within days Maria's parents had decided to sell up and move to Italy, taking their daughter and grandson with them. Maria was too ill to look after the child herself, and Matthew, despite his legal rights, was conveniently forgotten about.

Reaching the end of her story, Maria found she was weeping, and clutching the girl's hand so tightly, Lucie grimaced with pain.

'Sorry,' she said, releasing Lucie's hand and brushing away the tears.

For a few minutes, Lucie said nothing, as if trying to absorb the full implications of what she had been told. Maria knew Lucie wouldn't judge her, that was part of the unspoken agreement between them, but nevertheless she still seemed puzzled, as if there was still more to understand.

'Why didn't Matthew fight for David? How could he just let him go?' Lucie said at last. 'It seems so cruel— for both of them. A tiny child, unwanted by both his parents.'

'I don't know,' Maria replied sadly. 'I often wondered that in the years which followed. He had more right to the child than I did. I wish things could have been different.'

We all wish that,' Lucie said quietly, 'but it's an empty wish.

The past is what it is. Nothing can change that.'

And as if to prove the truth of her words, Lucie began to tell her own story, hesitantly, even fearfully, to begin with, but with growing confidence as she felt Maria's attention fixed on her, so steady and thoughtful, even at the most difficult moments.

It had got very cold on the hut and they had both wriggled inside their emergency sleeping bags, and made another hot drink. The storm still showed no sign of abating, and in a few hours it would be dark. Maria had tried contacting both the clinic and the hotel on her mobile phone, but the storm had disrupted the signal and they would have to wait for it to pass before they could hope to make contact. Their isolation was complete, and it favoured revelation.

Lucie's story was more one of hints and pauses, than a straightforward narrative, and it wasn't long before Maria was paying as much attention to what was unsaid, as said. A loved figure, friendly one minute, menacing the next, appeared again and again, among the broken words, like some recurring nightmare, lying in wait night after night. Sometimes the touches were so warm and comforting, she wanted to curl up and sleep, hugging the warmth to her like a worn doll. More often they were sharp and painful, an invasion she couldn't repel, and then a hand would be over her mouth and she would struggle to breathe. There was no stopping it. It went on and on down a dark tunnel of fear and shame, squeezing the life out of her, until there was nothing left. In the light she was silent, adrift from everyone else, except for the shadow which lurked in corners and smiled with the others. The pain of it all came through the long silences and tortured words, as if even to speak of it, was yet another violation.

When Lucie could say no more, Maria reached out her hand and touched her friend's face. A great sadness had settled on them both, but there was relief too.

For Lucie the unspeakable had been spoken and Maria had been witness to it.

For Maria, uncomfortable truths had been faced and accepted. A failure of love had betrayed her lover, her child and most of all herself, and redemption lay in facing the truth. The little which could be put right must be, and the rest left behind. The haunting was over, but the scars would remain.

Rescue came, as it often does, when least expected. Just as they were beginning to reconcile themselves to spending a long, cold, night in the hut, there was a loud banging on the door, the sound of men's voices, and the flash of a strong torch through the almost blocked window. Adrien had arrived with a couple of mountain guides to dig them out, and take them back to the clinic. He had been very concerned when the storm blew up, and there was no message from them, and he had set out at once to follow their route and search any hut on the way. For the last hour or so, the conditions had been so poor, they had made very slow progress, but Adrien had insisted they carry on.

'We couldn't let you spend a night out here,' he said smiling, as they repacked their rucksacks, tidied the hut and prepared to leave. 'Dr Williams would never have forgiven me.'

The snow had stopped when they emerged but the poles indicating the path had mostly disappeared. Adrien seemed unconcerned, he knew the route and the mountain so well. The three men were on skis and they had brought a sledge with them, piled with blankets, and big enough to carry both Maria and Lucie. The two girls looked at each other and smiled. They were cold and hungry but a great weight had been lifted from them both. The way back was going to be downhill and fast.

They couldn't wait.

* * *

Undeterred by their adventure, they took the path up the mountain many more times during the spring and summer of that year. They both became good mountain walkers, enjoying the challenge, but always respectful of the might they were up against. Their physical health improved enormously, and with it a contentment of mind which showed in both their faces. Lucie put on weight, and no longer lagged behind Maria on the steep sections of the path. Even as the sun strengthened, and the snow began its retreat, Maria did not flinch at the rising temperature. Her fear of the sun and its heat seemed a thing of the past, and instead she revelled in the long, summer days, which enabled her and Lucie to spend nearly all their spare time out of doors.

Dr Williams was delighted with the progress both young women had made. His experiment appeared to have been a great success, and he was duly congratulated by his colleagues. The friendship between Maria and Lucie grew stronger with each day which passed, and at every opportunity they would spend time together, walking and talking, as if no part of their lives past and present should remain a secret from the other. Their mutual dependence was obvious for all to see, and although Dr Williams rejoiced in the healing it brought, he soon began to worry about what would happen when their paths separated, as they surely would. After all, Maria had a child and parents she needed to return to, even a husband too, one day perhaps. The return to family was far less certain for Lucie, but she had her education to complete and arrangements were already being made by the guardian the court had appointed, for that to happen.

At the end of June, Maria had an unexpected visitor. Her parents had come regularly every month to the clinic to visit, but no one else. Summoned to Dr Williams' room, after lunch, one hot Sunday, he told her a young man had called to see her, without making an appointment, and was waiting in the visitors' room. She was not obliged to see him, but if she wanted to, it would be allowed.

'What's his name?' Maria asked, genuinely puzzled.

'Stephen,' replied Dr Williams. ' He said he was a relative of one of your neighbours in Italy.'

For a moment, Maria's mind wanted to block out the memory, but she wouldn't let it. She was stronger now, she could face it.

'Yes, I should like to see him very much,' she said simply. 'I remember him well.'

In the autumn, Maria was discharged. She had been in the clinic for just over fifteen months. Lucie had left at the end of August to pick up her education at the start of the academic year. The friends only had a few days warning, and then she was gone. If plans were made to keep in touch, they told no one about them, and their remaining few days together were spent walking on the mountain one last time. Looking at them both, on the eve of Lucie's departure, as they returned to the clinic, Dr Williams was struck by how much they had changed. The strain had gone from their faces and they no longer looked at the world with haunted eyes. There was still the odd moment of nervousness and uncertainty, but nothing which could really detract from the fact that they were now both well. The clinic had done its job, although how, where, and when, the cure had occurred precisely, was impossible to determine. Dr Williams felt justified in the approach he had taken, and that was all the satisfaction he needed.

Maria's parents didn't come to collect her from the clinic. She told them by letter that she didn't want to return home immediately, but was planning to stay with a friend in Geneva, and look for a job. She hoped they would be prepared to continue to look after David, and she would send for him when she was more settled.

Sally and Bernardo were very concerned but they couldn't stop her. Several years went by but Maria never did send for David or return home. To begin with, she would ring every two or three weeks, although the calls were always brief and factual, and didn't allow for casual chat, but as time went on they became more and more infrequent, until one day, silence. Their daughter had slipped beyond their reach and they knew she wanted it that way.

Two events act as an epilogue. A year or so after Maria left the clinic, the Gales sold their villa and returned to England. Before they left, they told Sally and Bernardo that their nephew Stephen had recently graduated from Oxford, and was now planning to marry, and emigrate to Canada, with his new wife. Toronto was mentioned as a possible destination, but nobody knew for sure.

IV. Matthew

He had no idea what made him change his mind. He had been so sensible during the winter months, despite a deep, inner, restlessness, which he found hard to control. Once or twice he caught Rosalind looking at him anxiously, as if she sensed the struggle he did his best to hide, but she said nothing. He knew she understood, but the battle was with himself.

His job, teaching English at the local secondary school, helped. He loved the work, and there was always more to do. His senior students were particularly keen and always grateful for any extra support he could give them, as they prepared for their exams. For the last few weeks, he had been giving some of them extra tutorials in the evening, often not returning to the flat until nine o'clock, in time for a late supper. Rosalind didn't seem to mind, as she was usually immersed in her own latest writing project, and only too glad of the extra time. Weekends, Matthew invariably kept free for his own research work, as he was planning to introduce a new course on The English Romantic Poets in the Autumn, and he wanted to get all his notes prepared before the summer season began on the river.

English Literature and kayaking were his two great

passions, and he had to forgo the latter entirely from October to May, when the river was unpredictable and dangerous, even for the most experienced kayaker. Matthew felt this deprivation keenly, the loss of a freedom he found only on the river, and on many occasions during the winter months, he was tempted to descend the narrow streets towards the river, rather than take the steep path up to the school, and the safety of academic study.

But he didn't. Despite the restless longing, which never left him, he was self-disciplined, and he knew the dangers. There might be a moment's hesitation but it was never more than that, before he turned his steps towards the school, eager to continue his reading or talk to his students. Once at school, he knew he was safe and he could gaze down over the grey, slate, roofs, towards the river, as it curved protectively around the village, with an almost detached pleasure. Intellectual challenge had always been important to him and made him a daring and inspirational teacher. In a similar way, the physical challenge, posed by the river, had enabled him to develop his kayaking skills to a very high level. Hard work and commitment had brought him an enviable expertise in both areas of his life, as Rosalind often reminded him.

'You are very lucky to be so good at the two things you love most,' she had said, as they relaxed after a late meal, one evening towards the end of February. 'I wish I could feel as happy with my writing.'

Matthew laughed. 'Writers always say that. Discontent is their natural state of being. You wouldn't be able to write at all if you weren't permanently dissatisfied.'

'I suppose that's true', Rosalind said ruefully, 'but I do envy you sometimes.'

'Well don't,' Matthew replied, getting up to refill their coffee cups. 'When you produce your masterpiece your satisfaction will far exceed anything I've ever felt, I'm sure of that.'

'Yes, but that might never happen,' Rosalind said, smiling. 'At least your achievement is here and now.'

'Well, let's talk about it again in ten years' time and then we'll see who's right.'

He kissed her on the top of the head, as he put her coffee cup down on the table in front of her.

'I've always believed in your talent, Ros, you know that. Why do you think I ran away with you?'

For a moment, the gently teasing tone in his voice disappeared as they both felt again the weight of what they had done.

Thinking back to that conversation, Matthew wondered if it had had anything to do with his change of mind. Had his comments really concealed a deep dissatisfaction with his own achievements, rather than a desire to encourage Rosalind in hers? He suspected he was being rather hard on himself, but he was desperate to find any reasonable justification for his actions. There were other reasons, of course, but they were so familiar, they didn't really count; the ongoing restlessness, always there beneath the surface, a weariness with the effort of self-discipline over so many long months, the temptation to test himself just a little bit more. On Saturday March 10th, for some unaccountable reason, they all came together and turned his feet in the wrong direction.

Of course, it didn't happen quite like that. Instead of acting on some spontaneous whim, there was something deliberate, even planned about what he did, although he would never have admitted it.

The day had started like any other Saturday, with no hint of what was to come, as they discussed their plans over breakfast. Rosalind was going into the local town with Luc to do the monthly shop for all the items the village was unable to supply, and she had arranged to meet Matthew at the hotel for lunch. It would be some weeks before the hotel opened for business again, but Matthew and Ros were treated like family, and always welcome. Matthew was to spend the morning in school, catching up on his marking and continuing to prepare his courses for the autumn. A walk on the Causse was planned for the afternoon, if the weather improved. It had been very wet and squally when they woke up and when Ros left, soon after breakfast, to walk to the hotel, the strength of the wind took her by surprise.

'You'll need a coat,' she shouted to Matthew, who was in the study, collecting things to take to school. 'It's pretty blustery out here. See you later.'

Last words and so ordinary, but then they often are.

Matthew heard Ros call out, caught the last few words, and then the door slammed shut, whipped back by a gust of wind, and she was gone.

For a few minutes he continued to sort out his books and papers. Then he stopped. His bag was open, on the chair, ready to be packed, but he left it there and walked into the kitchen, which doubled as a dining room. Their breakfast things were still on the small table under the window, and he piled them up, and carried them to the draining board, ready for the dishwasher.

At some level, a decision had been made and he went along with it, like a sleepwalker, unaware, yet precise and deliberate, in all his actions.

In the cupboard, next to the front door, was his kayaking kit, neatly stowed away for the winter. Several life jackets were piled on the floor, and an assortment of helmets hung from hooks on the back wall. Paddles of various lengths and weight were propped up in one corner, next to two barrels, for personal possessions, which were strapped to the back of the kayak on longer expeditions.

Matthew cast a quick, professional, eye over the kit, before selecting his newest life jacket and helmet, and the strongest of the double paddles. Stacking everything by the front door, he went into the bedroom to dress. The duvet had been pulled back but the bed wasn't made. There were dents in the pillows where their heads had been, and glancing at them, Matthew hesitated for a moment. A promise, about to be broken, hovered at the back of his mind, but then something shut down in his head, and he opened the wardrobe and reached for his wetsuit on the top shelf. He pulled an old tracksuit over the top and looked around in the bottom of the wardrobe for his trainers and a pair of thick socks. He would discard this outer layer when he got to the river, but he didn't want to be cold before he started.

Locking the front door behind him, he paused for a moment at the top of the steps which led down into the small square, in front of their flat. In summer it would be filled with tourists, eating at the small restaurant, a few doors along, which specialised in every type of crepes, or passing through the square on their way to what still remained of the abbey, and a wonderful view over the whole village and down the gorge towards the next village. Now the square was completely empty, the restaurant closed until the beginning of May, and the shutters, in varying shades of grey, green and orange, of the neighbouring houses, tightly shut to keep out the wind, which was gusting furiously down the narrow streets and whirling, like a demented dancer, in the small squares.

Up above, dark clouds raced towards the east, occasionally

letting through a sudden shaft of sunlight, as they were blown apart by the strong wind. Even on his own doorstep, high up in the village, Matthew could still hear the roar of the river as it tumbled over the weir, just beyond the hotel. A sudden surge of excitement left him feeling breathless and nervous at the same time, and he descended the steps quickly, before the buffeting wind could wrench the long paddle from his hands. An unacknowledged sense of guilt made him anxious not to meet anyone on his way to the river, and so he took the slightly longer route down the narrow, uneven, steps which came out near the front of the church. His luck held until just after the church, when he was about to cross the road, and head down towards the small, wooden, hut where they kept the kayaks.

Out of the wind, a voice, shouting. He tried to ignore it, but as he stepped on to the road, it came again, loud and insistent right behind him, and he felt obliged to turn round. It was Monsieur Badeaux, who owned one of the shops along the river front and had rented a room to them when they first came to the village. He was obviously agitated, gesturing wildly towards the paddle and other kit Matthew was carrying.

'Surely you are not going on the river?'

The words came to him, tossed by the wind, some barely audible.

'No, of course not,' Matthew mouthed back. The lie came so easily, it seemed like the truth. 'I'm just sorting some of my kit out—ready for next season.'

If Monsieur Badeaux heard the reply, he didn't register the fact.

'It's too dangerous. You mustn't go. The river is–' The last few words snatched away, as soon as they were uttered.

Matthew nodded, smiled at the anxious Frenchman, and crossing the road, lifted his hand in a friendly farewell.

Glancing back quickly from the other side, he could see that Monsieur Badeaux was still shouting, his arms going, like frantic windmills, but no sound reached him.

The river was very high and racing furiously through the gorge, the surface of the water whipped by the strong wind into a fine cloud of spray, which drifted across to him as he approached the shed, indistinguishable from the rain which had also begun to fall steadily since he left the flat.

Inside the small shed, he pulled the cover off his kayak, looking with pleasure at its sleek form and aware of the skilled engineering, which had gone into the construction of such a fine craft. The yellow paint, scrubbed clean the previous autumn, gleamed like a shaft of sunlight in the gloomy shed, and Matthew ran his fingers along the smooth, painted, surface with joyful appreciation.

Stripping off his tracksuit, he put on his life jacket and helmet and looked around for his rubber shoes and the spare paddle he always kept in the shed for emergencies. Slipping it into the well of the kayak, he wedged the door of the shed open and picked up the rope to pull the kayak down to the water's edge. Once again, for a few seconds, in the darkened shed, something stirred at the back of his mind, urging him towards caution and common sense, but the restless longing was too strong and the roar of the river obliterated all thoughts of fear and danger.

Matthew's practised eye looked carefully for the best launching point. In the winter the river changed so dramatically all previous points of reference were lost, and Matthew had to look afresh at its movement and the contours of the bank. Spotting a new, shallow, inlet the river had made, in its relentless erosion of the shingle bank, some fifty metres down from the hut, Matthew dragged the kayak towards it. He knew that as soon as it was on the water, the wind would seize the kayak, and either turn it over or whisk it down the river. He would have to wait for a lull in the wind, and then move very swiftly.

Checking that his helmet was on firmly and his life jacket fastened correctly, he waited patiently for the right moment. Nothing existed but the pounding of the river as it tore along beside him, the thudding of his own heart, and the tension of taut muscles, ready to spring into action.

On the water, the wind was gusting so strongly from east to west, it took him some minutes to get a feel for the current. For all its superior engineering, the kayak was so light, the wind tossed it about as carelessly as a leaf. Matthew dug deep with the paddle to steady it, as he caught the current mid- stream, his eyes scanning the river ahead, for any sign of familiar rocks, now mostly submerged beneath the turbulent water. The kayak was made of Kelvar, a very strong, durable, material and was designed to resist a severe battering, but Matthew knew that if its bottom was ripped out, it would be hard for him to survive in the raging waters.

A lull in the wind gave him a breathing space as he directed the kayak towards a race of tumbling water, just before the old Roman bridge, which spanned the river at the southern end of the village. He knew all the rapids, their quirks and dangers, so intimately they usually held no fear for him, but this was different. The old landmarks had gone, the safest course could be little more than guesswork, and all the time the wind threatened to fling him aside from his chosen route.

Fortunately, his kayak was so light it skimmed the surface of the water, like a bird swooping for insects, and only grazed itself slightly on the sharp rocks just below the surface. Below the bridge, the river slowed a little in its headlong course, and he felt the kayak respond more readily to his paddle, as he propelled it down a long, straight, stretch of the river, usually glassy calm during the summer months.

Luc had laughed when he protested that a river has moods, as varied and unpredictable as any human being, accusing him of fanciful, emotional nonsense, born of his crazy infatuation with an inanimate force of nature.

'You will be saying the river has a spirit next,' he jested, enjoying his friend's confusion 'as well as sticks and stones and whatever else you care to mention. You've been reading too much Romantic poetry Matthew, that's the trouble. A good dose of realism would put you straight'.

At the time, he had taken this teasing in good part, but now, recollecting the conversation, he smiled grimly to himself. There was nothing more real than the challenge he was facing now, self-inflicted though it was. Every moment was a battle against elements which seemed determined to overcome him and his frail craft. The river, a much loved companion, in its quieter moments, now seemed set to push him to his utmost limits, as the wind and rain added their strength to the test he was facing.

In the absence of any immediate hazard, and with the kayak on a reasonably steady course down the middle of the river, Matthew had the opportunity to look around him, and try to gauge just how high the river had risen with the spring flood. Such an estimate would help him to navigate a trickier part of the river, just before the next village, where there were a series of rapids, which could be difficult to deal with even during the summer months, when the river was relatively low and quiet. If the river had risen any more than a metre many of the familiar rocks would now be submerged, and the safe passage through a rapid could be completely different. Looking at the rock face, as the current swept him rapidly onward, Matthew guessed the river had, in fact, probably risen nearer three metres, drowning caves and waterfalls and altering the whole look of the gorge as he knew it.

Disorientated by this distortion of the familiar, he sometimes lost all sense of where he was on the river, as if in some dream world, where nothing was quite as he expected. Things were made worse by the stinging spray, which forced him to keep his eyes closed and his head down, the bow of the kayak, the limit of his vision. Usually, he found it easy to tell when he was approaching a rapid or turbulent stretch of water, from the familiar roar and line of white foam in the distance, but under extreme conditions, all such indications were lost.

Around him, water surged and crashed against the mighty rock faces, and it took every ounce of his strength just to keep the kayak upright and moving forwards. Sudden gusts of wind sounded strangely like the roar of a rapid, which left him peering through the rain and spray, in a state of perpetual readiness for that plunge through racing water, and the desperate struggle to avoid unknown rocks as they loomed up, like black ghosts, through a curtain of white, so dense, he marvelled that he could pass through it.

Terrified and exhilarated by turn, Matthew experienced every moment with an intensity which was almost painful. Alert to every danger, and yet powerless in the hands of a force which left him so little control, he felt emptied of the restlessness which had plagued him for so long and rejoiced in his defiance. Every sensation came to him with a vividness and sharpness which made him shout out loud, as the kayak leapt through the tumbling water, or was swept irresistibly towards the rock face.

The need for constant vigilance and the tremendous physical strain left Matthew's mind surprisingly free. Never before had he felt the separation of mind and body so completely. While his body registered every physical sensation and reacted instinctively to the dangers around him, his mind summoned images of the past, like someone, relaxed and unhurried, sifting through a pile of old photographs. Certain faces, like portraits in an exhibition, appeared again and again, at different ages and in different settings. His son David, in a pushchair, bundled up against the cold, his small, round face peeping out from his woolly hat. Was that the last time he saw him? He couldn't be sure. The older David couldn't be summoned; he didn't know him and probably never would. His father, leaning over his shoulder, to read an essay he had written on Hamlet, and picking out all the spelling mistakes as he did so. And Rosalind.

Again and again, Rosalind's face blotted out everything else, too alive and insistent, to be a memory yet, and always on the point of saying something, but then gone before the words could come. Tears and smiles, questions and uncertainty, passed over her face, like clouds across the sun, and his heart contracted with love and guilt. And Maggie too, as he had seen her when he first came to Layters school for an interview all those years ago, her expression welcoming, sympathetic and a little conspiratorial, even then. And the same face shocked and tearful, witnessing a love she didn't want to see. There was another image too, of course, but it wouldn't come. It was buried too deep and it made his heart ache.

People and places, that's what we remember, but for Matthew people won every time. Places were background, it was the people which caught at his heart, except for the river, always the river, although as friend or destroyer, it was still uncertain.

It was thirteen kilometres to the next village, and Matthew guessed he had already covered ten of them. If so, he knew he must be approaching the series of very tricky, even dangerous rapids in the winter season, which came very quickly, one after another, as the river twisted its way through the narrowing gorge towards the next village.

Every now and then he would look upward, through a mist of blown rain and spray, searching for one particular rock formation which had so delighted Rosalind on one of their earliest trips down the river together. From a certain angle, two rocks, carved so expertly by wind and rain, became the perfect representation of a mother and child. The larger of the two rocks, the mother, appeared to have a shawl or scarf draped over her head and shoulders, and she was bending towards the smaller rock, the child, who looked to be carrying a basket. Something in the mother's posture seemed to suggest she was anxious to see what the basket contained, or was she just going to place a kiss on the child's head? Rosalind was captivated by the figures who appeared to have sprung, whole and lifelike from the very top of the gorge, and seemed so at ease in their perilous position. In her excitement, she lost control of her kayak for a few moments and the river pounced. She was never in any real danger, but it taught them both a lesson. A moment's lapse in concentration and the river could be merciless.

Now, Matthew needed a sighting of the two figures so he could be certain of his place on the river. It was startling how different the gorge looked with three more metres of water in it, and it made it very difficult for him to judge just how near he was to the next rapid. The wind and rain also distorted sound as well as obscuring his vision, as he searched for well-known landmarks. It was vital, therefore, that he kept alert for those rock formations the rising river couldn't alter.

He nearly missed them. He had lowered his head to protect himself from another violent gust of wind and the ferocious lash of whipped spray, and when he did venture to look up again they were just beginning to disappear behind him. He only caught a glimpse, before he felt the current accelerate beneath his kayak, which then swung broadside to the river and began to drift swiftly down a wide race of foaming water. An icy hand gripped his heart as he recognised the place, and every instinct for survival leapt to attention. His mind was clear, as he felt again the warmth of that hot, summer's day, barely two weeks after their arrival in the village. They had taken to the river to escape the stuffy oppression of their rented room, with a sense of release, which had filled them both with joy. Every moment was intensified by their love and sense of freedom, and lasting happiness seemed within their grasp. When Rosalind lost control of her kayak he hadn't been particularly alarmed, and had even found her predicament, wedged against the rock face by a relentless current, rather comical. They both treated the incident lightly, but nevertheless it had felt like a warning.

Now roles were reversed and there was no-one to laugh and call out to him as he fought the full force of the river, intent on sweeping him towards the towering wall of limestone, which plunged into the raging water ahead of him. Straining every muscle to the utmost, Matthew tried to swing the kayak round, so that he could guide it past the rock face, and out into the middle of the river again.

Every second seemed an hour as the bow inched slowly round, but the current was too strong, and he knew he wouldn't make it. To his surprise, he felt no sense of panic, as he waited for the inevitable impact, just an overwhelming feeling of relief that if this was to be the end, at least it was on the river. It seemed as if he had made a deliberate choice, and yet behind that thought, there were stirrings of regret and guilt, and a deep love of life which brought tears to his eyes.

The impact knocked him out, as he caught a glancing blow from the rock face just above his right eye. Slipping from the kayak, as it tipped on its side, his body surrendered, without a murmur, to the violent suck of the current as it dived into the cave under the overhang of rock, dragging its prey with it. The flash of yellow remained like a beacon on the surface for other eyes to find, while the river raced on southwards, unburdened and uncaring.

V. Rosalind

She must have been gazing out of the window when the letter came. It hadn't been there, in the post box, when she came back from the shops. She'd checked. Since then she hadn't done much, except gaze out of the window. She hadn't even felt inclined to unpack the shopping. It could all wait. Then something had prompted her to go down and look in the post box again. She didn't know what, just a feeling she had. And there it was, in the post box, on its own, as if someone had dropped it in casually while passing. For a moment or two she hesitated. She couldn't see the writing, the envelope was face down, and she might be wrong. To delay any possible disappointment, she took the letter out of the box without looking at it, clutching it in her left hand as she shut and relocked the box.

Back in the flat, she left the letter on the table, still address down, and went back to gazing out of the window. She had done so much of it lately; it helped her to think. She had sent the letter to Maggie several weeks ago, she couldn't remember exactly how many. Time had taken on a different character since Matthew's death, less controllable somehow, and with a tendency to stretch out or contract in a most bizarre fashion. She had left, what she thought was a decent interval, before she sent the manuscript. She had wanted to give Maggie time to adjust. After all, her letter, coming out of the blue, as it did, was probably a bit of a shock. A teacher, hearing from a student, after seventeen years, was unusual enough in itself, but after what had happened to them, it bordered on the traumatic. In fact, she had not been quite accurate when she had said at the end of the letter, 'It's on its way to you now' as the final draft was still on the computer, waiting to be printed out. Still the words were an intention rather than a fact, a truth postponed, as she did send it less than three weeks later.

It was a sunny, fresh morning, and you could feel summer just round the corner, when she walked down to the village post office, the parcel, carefully wrapped and sealed, under her arm. For some reason, she felt quite nervous, even reluctant, about letting the parcel out of her hands, and she still held on to it very firmly as she asked the girl behind the desk about the different postal rates.

'I suggest you have it signed for-- if it's important or valuable,' the girl said briskly, noticing Rosalind's obvious reluctance to part with the parcel.

'Thank you I will,' Rosalind said gratefully, pushing the parcel under the raised grille, with a sudden, decisive movement. 'How long will it take to get there?'

'Anything up to a week,' the girl replied, glancing quickly at the address, as she stuck stamps on and handed Rosalind something to sign.

'Thank you. That's fine,' Rosalind said lightly, embarrassed about appearing too possessive about the parcel. 'It's not urgent but I just want to make sure it gets there.'

'Oh, it will do that all right,' the girl said, with confident efficiency. 'Don't worry about that. Anyway, you can always track it on our website. You've got the bit of paper.'

And that was it. The girl threw the parcel into a large sack just behind her, and it was on its way.

Since that morning she had spent quite a lot of each day gazing out of the window, and now with the arrival of the long awaited and longed for reply to her letter and parcel, she was still doing it. The letter lay unopened on the table behind her, as she gazed down, yet again, over the grey, slate, roofs, towards the river, taking deep, regular, breaths to calm herself and clear her head.

The view was so familiar, so soothing in a way, and yet it also had the power to provoke such powerful emotions, as her heart ached with the weight of memories it conjured up. She couldn't see much of the river from where she was standing, only the glint of light on water, as it curved southwards, beyond the old Roman bridge, but it was enough. It was the river which had filled Matthew's mind and heart during those last few hours, and it was the river, and only the river, which could bring him close to her again.

She knew now she would never go back. At one time, just after she finished writing the book, she thought she might. She even entertained the idea of presenting Maggie with a copy in person, but soon realised such a fantasy was only the result of the sudden elation she had felt on finally completing the book. That moment of euphoria soon evaporated, however, and although she was still left with the strong desire to contact Maggie and give her the book, she knew she wouldn't leave the village to do so. In a sense, she was as much a prisoner of the gorge, as the Saint had been, and only in the acceptance of that fate, would she find some peace.

Now a reply had come from the past and she must prepare herself for all the upheaval that could bring. She was convinced the letter was from Maggie, although she hadn't yet dared to look at the handwriting. Of course, there was just a chance she wouldn't recognise it, but then someone's handwriting doesn't usually change that much, even over time. For a student, a teacher's handwriting becomes loaded with meaning far beyond the words actually written. Every comment has the power to bring joy or despair, and is so closely involved in the student's own feelings of success and failure. Rosalind had treasured Maggie's comments, written in pencil at the bottom of her essays, extracting from them all the motivation she needed to keep on reading, and thinking, and writing. The shape of those words were engraved on her mind; surely she couldn't fail to recognise them?

The address was printed, not hand written, but the stamp was British. Disappointment, doubt, and then relief followed each other, as she ripped open the envelope and saw the familiar handwriting. There wasn't much of it, the note was very brief, but it immediately took her back nearly twenty years. Like her student self, savouring the moment before she read the longed for comment at the foot of her essay, she paused before allowing the meaning of the words, written so neatly, on the thin sheet of blue paper, to sink in. The brevity of the letter suggested rejection, and she readied herself to take the blow, but there was none. The note, for it was really no more than that, made her heart pound with excitement and apprehension as there was no hint of rejection, in fact the opposite was true, and not at all what she had expected:

Dear Ros, (the informality of the greeting whisked away the years and squeezed at her heart).
It was a wonderful surprise to hear from you after so many years, and it has thrown my life into turmoil! The letter and manuscript arrived safely and it's taken me a little time to adjust

to both. The news about Matthew was a terrible shock and I have thought so much about the pain you must be suffering. I know something of that grief myself.

One good thing, however, has come out of such a tragedy. David, Matthew's son, has been in touch and we have met. He is a fine, young man, and so like Matthew.

It would make your heart ache to see him. So that is what we are going to do. We are coming to see you. I feel it is the only way to make peace with the past and I hope you agree.

I know this is presumptuous but we have booked two seats on the flight to Rodez in two weeks' time, on June 15th. The flight gets in at 6.30pm and I was wondering if you could arrange for someone to meet us. I have also booked two rooms in a local hotel, it may well be the one you mentioned in your letter. The proprietor's name is Grenier, although I think it was the son I spoke to on the phone.

I know we are taking a risk Ros, but I believe you will understand why. There are things the three of us still need to face and forgive, and the gorge which Matthew obviously loved so much, is probably the place to do it. Let's hope so.

With warmest good wishes,
Maggie.

Minutes turned into half an hour as Rosalind, letter in hand, allowed the past to wash over her, like a giant wave, sucking her back into the sea of emotion which had deposited her and Matthew in the gorge so many years ago.

Maggie was right, of course, Rosalind had no doubt about that, but, nevertheless, the boldness of the move startled her.

It would be hard enough facing Maggie after what they had done, but David, Matthew's lost son, how was she going to deal with that? Immediately after Matthew's death she had desperately wanted to contact David, but had done nothing. It had all seemed too difficult and Luc had discouraged her. The guilt remained, however, and was added to the other fear, which had lurked at the back of her mind ever since the day Matthew had run away with her, and abandoned his son for ever. What was David going to feel about the woman who had deprived him of his father for so long? She was surprised, even a little shocked, that he had agreed to come at all. He must be full of anger and resentment against her. How had Maggie managed it? The meeting would be more than awkward and she was not sure she could face it, whatever Maggie said. Sometimes the right thing to do just wasn't possible, and they might all have to accept that. And yet, despite the fear and guilt, something leapt in her heart at the thought of coming face to face with a part of Matthew she had never known. Catharsis—pity and fear. Didn't she need that cleansing if she was to go on? Maggie obviously thought so, and there was good reason to trust her. The betrayal had been theirs, and Maggie had paid a heavy price for it.

It was three days before Rosalind replied to the letter, and then it was only a brief email. She had noticed there was an email address printed neatly below the scrawl of Maggie's signature, and she jotted it down at once in the address book, in case she lost the letter. Matthew had always known Maggie's postal address, and it was one of only a very few addresses they had kept a note of during all their years in the gorge, but he had never mentioned an email address. It didn't matter at the time when they were keen to sever all contacts with the past, but now she was grateful that it was so quick and easy to get in touch.

She also needed time. Time to think, and time to talk to Luc, before she replied. Fortunately, it was early in the season and the hotel wasn't too busy so she knew Luc would be free most of the afternoon. She would walk down and see him after lunch.

Putting the letter in her bag, she unpacked the shopping, and then spent the rest of the morning cleaning and tidying the flat.

Luc had just finished clearing the last of the lunch tables when she arrived and was pleased to see her. Fetching two glasses of wine from the bar, they went out onto the terrace, choosing a table at the far end, where there was a good view of the gorge and no chance of being disturbed.

Luc had sensed immediately Rosalind's restless excitement and guessed something important had happened. Ever since Matthew's death, he had kept a protective eye on the young widow but had refused to let himself get too close. He knew he would be in danger if he did. Once, many years before, he had let his feelings show, and he had vowed never to let it happen again. It had been a mistake then and it would be a mistake now. Rosalind was still grieving for Matthew, and so was he. Friendship was as far as they could go.

Seated, they sipped their wine in silence for a few minutes, enjoying each other's company and the warmth of the early summer sun. The sound of the river, still quite full from the late spring rains, filled the air as it poured over the weir, just upstream from the hotel. Luc knew how difficult Rosalind still found it sometimes to listen to the river and he glanced anxiously at her as they drank. Aware of Luc's concern, she smiled and reached across the table to touch his hand.

'It's all right, Luc. Today it's definitely all right.'

Puzzled, but relieved, he looked at her inquiringly.

'What is it, Ros? Something's happened. Tell me.'

'I've had a letter. It came this morning from Maggie, and I need your help.'

'You mean Maggie Pool, your teacher—Matthew's colleague, that Maggie?'

As he spoke, Luc leaned across the table and grasped both of Rosalind's hands in his.

'Yes, yes of course. Who else?' Rosalind replied, gripping his hands tightly in her excitement. She had had the letter for several hours but what it contained, what it meant was only just beginning to sink in.

'They are coming to visit me, Luc. Maggie and Matthew's son, David, are coming here, to the gorge, to see me.'

Rosalind gave a little gasp, like a strangled sob, and tears filled her eyes.

'When? How?' Luc said quickly. 'And why now?'

'I don't know,' Rosalind replied. 'Perhaps David's just found out about his father. Maggie met him. I know that.'

'What a bombshell!' Luc said, getting up and moving to sit next to Rosalind. He put an arm round her shoulders and kissed her gently on the forehead.

'You're not on your own, Ros. You know that. I'll do whatever I can to help.'

Over the next two weeks, Luc and Rosalind met much more frequently than usual. Rosalind needed to talk and Luc felt bound to listen. He had heard most of it before, particularly during the long evenings the three of them had spent together in those early years in the gorge, when both Matthew and Rosalind had felt a strong desire to tell their friend everything. On those occasions, the lovers had shared the telling of their story, one picking up naturally, from where the other left off. Inevitably, some things had been suppressed, left unsaid, but now things were different. One of the narrators was dead, the other left to make sense of the story in whatever way she could, and very soon she would have two, new, voices to help her.

Luc had heard enough about Maggie and David for them to exist as more than names in his head. In some ways, his knowledge of them was surprisingly intimate, and yet he had no picture of them in his mind, to attach his knowledge to.

'I suppose you will recognise Maggie all right?' He had said one evening when Rosalind had invited him to the flat for supper. It was a Sunday evening, when the restaurant at the hotel was fairly quiet, and he knew his parents would be able to cope on their own.

'Yes, I'm sure of that,' Rosalind replied. 'She made such an impression on me as a student, a schoolgirl. I could never forget her face.'

'She must have been an exceptional teacher,' Luc said thoughtfully. 'You obviously loved and admired her very much.'

For a second or two, a shadow hovered over Rosalind's face 'Yes, I did. But we made life very difficult for her, Matthew and I. I can see that clearly now. It really wasn't fair.'

She spoke quietly and sadly, ashamed to look Luc in the eye, although she knew he wouldn't judge her.

'It was a long time ago, Ros. I'm sure she's forgiven you by now,' he replied, after a a moment or two. 'After all she obviously wants to see you again, that must be a good sign.'

'I hope so,' Rosalind said, a little hesitantly, 'or maybe she is just coming to hold David's hand.'

'Maybe she is, but I'll be there to hold yours,' Luc said, smiling. 'So stop worrying. Remember it's Matthew's son we're talking about. A young man who just needs to fill in some missing parts of the jigsaw, and who can blame him?'

On that occasion, and on several others, during what seemed a very long two weeks, Luc steadied her nerves and helped her to see things in a more rational light. He never belittled her fears and anxieties, but he also refused to let her make too much of them.

He had agreed immediately to Rosalind's request to take her to Rodez airport, to meet Maggie and David off their flight on the 15th. He was also pleased the visitors had booked rooms at the hotel, as it should enable him to take some pressure off Rosalind in the coming days. If David was coming with the intention of wreaking revenge on his father's lover, he would have him to deal with first.

Rosalind woke early on the morning of June 15th and she knew at once that the weather had changed. The bedroom was gloomy, and when she opened the shutters, she could see heavy clouds shrouding the top of the gorge, or drifting in lazy wisps towards the river below. The air was unusually cool and she shivered slightly as she pulled off her thin, night shirt and dressed quickly in cotton trousers and a T-shirt. Luc had arranged to take most of the day off, and had promised to be at the flat in time for coffee.

The plan was to drive to Rodez for lunch and do some shopping, before driving out to the airport, in the late afternoon, to meet the 6.30 flight from Stansted. Beyond that her mind wouldn't go, and for the moment she was grateful. Meanwhile she still had to finish what she had started the previous evening, and she had just enough time to do so.

In the study, the desk was completely covered with photographs, going right back to 2012, when her affair with Matthew had started. Most of the photographs, taken in 2012, were of the Haworth trip and invariably included either Matthew or Maggie, or both of them, surrounded by a group of eager, enthusiastic, girls. She hadn't used her phone but a conventional camera her parents had given her for her sixteenth birthday, and she was glad of that now. If the pictures had been on the phone, they would have been long gone, but instead she still had tangible proof of her memories, whenever she wanted to revisit them. She hadn't done so very often, but it was strangely comforting to know she could if she wished. During their early years in the gorge, she had had no desire to look at photographs which reminded her of a past they had turned their backs on, but as time went on, and certainly after Matthew's death, she had returned to them several times, as she tried to make sense of what had happened. And it had helped, making the connection between past and present in such a visual way. Maybe it would do the same for David. Anyway she wanted to be prepared.

The majority of the photographs, of course, were of the village and the gorge. There were countless pictures of Matthew kayaking, with one or two of both of them, taken by some willing bystander, and a few of Rosalind alone, although she had always been a reluctant subject. Matthew had changed very little in appearance over the years, as if the gorge or rather the river, had bestowed on him the gift of everlasting youth. Placing two pictures of him, side by side, taken fifteen years apart, it was almost impossible to tell which was the earliest. The same restless excitement shone out of his eyes in every photograph, as if he was always looking to move on, to continue the escape. During the fifteen months since his death, Rosalind had found it almost unbearable to look at the most recent photographs they had taken, afraid to discover that a shadow already hung over them. However, when she did steel herself to take a quick glance, the same Matthew, teasingly alive, soon dispersed her fears and laughed at her folly.

The photographs laid out on the desk were the final selection. It had taken Rosalind most of the previous evening to choose the ones she thought would interest David the most, and Maggie too perhaps. They would only tell part of the story, of course, but it was what she could offer. David would have to look elsewhere for insight into his father's earliest years. As far as she knew his grandfather was still alive, although already lost in the grip of dementia, but his grandmother had died from breast cancer more than six years before. It was not going to be easy for the young man to fill in the gaps, and her heart ached for his loss. Whatever his feelings towards her might be, they would surely be as one in their grief, and that was a comfort of sorts.

In the third drawer of the desk, which was deeper than the rest, there were two photograph albums they had been given as presents and never used. Rosalind guessed they would be just big enough to hold all the photographs she had selected, with a few pages left, in case David wanted to add some of his own, after the visit.

It took Rosalind over an hour to fill the two albums. Before she slipped a photograph into its transparent pocket, she wrote brief details of what, who, when, and where, on the back, so the collection would tell a more coherent story for anyone who bothered to look. The whole task was very satisfying, and helped a little to settle the flutters of alarm in her stomach, as she thought of the day ahead.

At 10.30 there was a loud knock on the front door, a cheerful shout of greeting, and the sound of a key turning in the lock. Rosalind had given Luc a key soon after Matthew's death, and although he rarely used it, she felt more secure as a result.

Luc noticed the albums as soon as he came in.

'I haven't seen one of these for years,' he said smiling. 'You have been busy.'

'I thought David might like them. Help him to know a bit

more about his father. Anyway they are there if he wants them.'

'A very kind gesture,' Luc said quietly. 'He would be a fool not to treasure them.'

Sympathy at that moment was too much. Without warning, huge sobs shook Rosalind, and she sat down heavily on the nearest chair.

'I'm sorry Luc. It suddenly all got too much. I'll be okay in a moment.'

Luc knelt down in front of her and put his arms round her waist.

'This is a big moment Ros, and possibly a difficult one. Tears are to be expected.'

Without intending to, and to her own surprise, Ros bent down towards Luc's upturned face and kissed him firmly on the lips, her tears wetting his cheeks, as he pulled her very close.

When they broke apart, they were both blushing, but they said nothing. Memory of another kiss intensified the feeling between them and words were unnecessary.

'Do you want a coffee?' Rosalind asked, retreating to the bathroom to wash her face, 'or do you want to get going?'

'Well, it's at least a two hour drive. Probably best to start as soon as possible. I've booked somewhere a bit special for lunch, so we mustn't be late.'

It could have been a much-looked-forward-to, relaxed day out, and yet it wasn't. On the drive to Rodez they hardly spoke, both too preoccupied with their own thoughts, and when it came to lunch, neither of them had much of an appetite. Rosalind tried to eat something as she knew Luc had gone to some trouble to book the table, but she couldn't finish her main course and she declined a sweet.

'We'll have to come another time,' she said consolingly,

sensing Luc's disappointment. 'Today everything is difficult. I'm sorry.'

'Not your fault,' he replied gruffly. 'It's got to me as well. Another day it will be different.'

Comforted by their mutual understanding, they paid the bill and left. Luc had a list of things he needed to buy for the hotel which kept them occupied for an hour or two before they returned to the car, and headed out of town towards the airport.

It had remained overcast all day, and not long after they left the outskirts of Rodez behind, it began to rain quite heavily.

'Not the best weather for a first visit to the gorge,' Luc said wryly. 'Let's hope it clears up later.'

Rosalind nodded in agreement, a solid knot of apprehension making her feel slightly nauseous

'Are you okay?' Luc asked, noticing how pale she had gone under her light tan.

'It's not far now but we can stop if you like.'

'No, let's just get there,' Rosalind said brusquely. 'It's nearly six.'

Ten minutes later they reached a small roundabout and turned off it towards a long, low, building, with a control tower at one end, which had emerged suddenly out of the mist and rain. The car park was tiny, and they had difficulty finding a space, every delay making Rosalind feel even more on edge.

The airport had very few facilities, and nowhere comfortable to wait. They scanned the Arrivals board anxiously to check the flight was on time. There were still twenty minutes until it was due, but to their surprise it flashed up as already landed.

'That's good,' Luc said cheerfully. 'At least we won't have to hang around for long. They should be through in a few minutes.'

For Rosalind, it all seemed like some strange dream, and she had to struggle hard to hang on to any sense of reality. In a matter of moments, she would be face to face with two people, both strangers now in their different ways, and yet so important to her for all that. It was an odd, disorientating, situation to be in, and she felt hot with unfamiliar shyness. She was glad Luc was with her, she couldn't have managed without him, but it should have been Matthew who was standing next to her and waiting for his son. The pain of his loss seemed to surround her like a reproach, making her own grief, as fresh and sharp, as on the day he died.

Contrary to what she had expected, it was David she spotted first. With a shock of recognition, which made her catch her breath, he caught her notice as soon as he came through the swing doors from Arrivals. It was something about the way he walked, head down, and shoulders slightly hunched, which made her heart stop, and for a moment the years rolled back, and Matthew, her teacher and lover, was again walking across the school courtyard towards her. The likeness between father and son was far greater than anything she had imagined, and it shook her to the core.

David hadn't recognised her, of course, and was looking anxiously at the crowd gathered to greet the flight, for some clue as to which one of them was the woman who had stolen his father from him so many years before. He was pulling two cases, and every now and then, turned to speak to someone who was following close behind him.

For a minute or two, Rosalind had no clear view of his companion, and then suddenly there she was, Maggie, walking out of a past, which seemed like yesterday. Her hair was grey and her face a little more lined, but otherwise she was unchanged. If she had been accompanied by a crowd of girls, hanging on her every word, Rosalind wouldn't have been surprised. The same, thoughtful, eager, look lit up her face, and she smiled encouragingly, whenever the young man turned to speak to her.

'There they are,' Rosalind said in a hoarse whisper, clutching at Luc's sleeve.

'The young man and the woman with grey hair; that's Maggie and David.'

At the very moment she spoke, Luc had also caught sight of David and was shocked by the likeness. Matthew, as he had first known him, was back from the dead. The accident had never happened.

Taking a deep breath, he made a great effort to readjust to reality, and stepped forward from the crowd to greet the young man.

'Hello. I'm Luc Grenier and you must be David Farr. It's a great pleasure to meet you. Welcome to France.'

Rosalind, hovering just behind Luc, barely registered Luc's words, her attention focused on David's companion, who was looking at her with such delight and concern, she felt a lump come in her throat and her eyes filled with tears.

'Hello Ros. How are you? It's so good to see you.'

Maggie gave Rosalind a quick, reassuring hug, before taking her hand and turning to speak to David.

'David, this is Rosalind, your father's partner, and a very talented ex-student of mine.'

With some obvious reluctance, the young man moved forward to shake the hand Rosalind offered, his mouth set in a hard line, as if he was desperate to suppress any emotion.

'Pleased to meet you,' he muttered, almost inaudibly, releasing Rosalind's hand quickly as if he'd been stung.

Rosalind's worst fears were confirmed. It was a mistake to revisit the past, and she should never have agreed to such a meeting. David was clearly unhappy about the whole thing, and still full of anger and resentment against her. Who could blame him? Rosalind thought, as they all moved, in a group, towards the exit, Luc leading the way with Maggie, while she and David followed in silence. In his eyes, she was the scarlet woman, the temptress, the precocious schoolgirl, who had compromised her susceptible young teacher. No wonder he hated her, she would have felt the same. She sighed inwardly. The truth was so different, but there was no sign he would be prepared to believe it.

Walking beside him to the car, a strange misery enveloped her. In appearance and mannerisms, the young man was the image of his father, and she felt a stab of raw grief, which made her catch her breath with the pain. It could have been Matthew next to her, and yet it wasn't. Matthew was gone. Their life together was gone, and there was nothing the young man, striding sullenly beside her, could do about that. When they reached the car there was a moment's confusion about who should sit where, until David resolved it, by sliding into the seat next to Luc, and leaving the back for the two women.

The light was fading as they drove off into the dull, rainy, evening and for once Rosalind felt no surge of excitement at the thought of introducing new visitors to the beauty and power of her beloved gorge.

In making arrangements for the visit, Maggie had made no mention of how long she and David were planning to stay, and it soon became clear that she had left things open deliberately. She knew that they would all need time to get used to the situation, and that acceptance and reconciliation would not come easily. It also hadn't taken long for her to realise what a support Luc was to Rosalind, and that she would be able to rely on him to help her guide Rosalind through the tricky waters ahead. She was immediately attracted to his wise and level headed approach to things and very relieved they had booked rooms in his hotel. He had informed her, on the night they arrived, that the rooms were at their disposal for as long as they wished and that there would be no charge. Maggie tried to protest against such generosity but Luc was adamant. It was early in the season, there was no pressure on rooms and, as friends of Rosalind, they were guests not punters.

During the following days, Maggie had plenty of opportunity to observe the love the young hotelier obviously felt for Rosalind, and she was glad. It was time Rosalind had someone new in her life, although Maggie found it harder to tell whether she returned Luc's feelings, with the same passion and intensity. She certainly depended on him, that was quite clear, but for the moment was struggling with too many other emotions, to allow love free reign. Maggie guessed other things needed to be settled first, before Rosalind could contemplate the future. With this hope, a lurking fear that the visit to the gorge had been rash and ill advised disappeared, and despite the tension still existing between them all, she began to feel a lot more optimistic.

From the moment David arrived in the gorge, he was anxious to visit all of his father's old haunts, and he chose Luc as his guide. Rosalind was upset by his continued coldness towards her, but not surprised. It was an emotional time for the young man and she understood his pain. Maggie could see how hurt Rosalind was, and on the third evening of their visit she tackled David about it, as they were walking back to the hotel, from Rosalind's flat, after having had supper with her and Luc.

'I wish you could make your peace with Rosalind,' she said quietly, glancing at David, as they made their down the narrow streets, towards the river. 'She loved your father very much, and it's tearing her apart to feel that his son hates her, and wants to keep her at such a distance.'

'I don't hate her,' David replied quickly, almost angrily. 'I don't know what I feel about her. She had all those years with my father and I didn't. It just doesn't seem fair somehow.'

'It wasn't fair but it also wasn't planned,' Maggie said firmly. 'Your father didn't want to lose touch with you, I'm sure of that, and it certainly wasn't Rosalind's fault if he did. Things happen. Nobody wants them to but they do.'

David nodded but said nothing.

'You seem to have forgiven me. Can't you do the same for Rosalind?' Maggie continued, after a pause. 'She's suffering too, you know. I imagine it is as hard for her to have you here, as it is for you to be here.'

'I know,' David said, a slight tremor in his voice, as he struggled to control his feelings. 'But you both had so much more of my father than I did. If he loved me, I was too young to remember his love. It's as if I've been carrying round a big, empty, hole all my life and now I'm trying to fill it, but it's not really working.'

'Why don't you let Rosalind help you?' Maggie said gently, touching David's arm.

'I think she's probably the only one who can. Luc can show you the river, which your father loved, and where he spent so much of his time, but Rosalind can bring you closer to the man. Give her a chance David, for both your sakes.'

David said nothing, and when they reached the hotel, they parted without another word. Maggie wondered if she had pushed too hard, but something had to give if the healing was to start.

It didn't take Rosalind and Maggie long to adjust to their new relationship. At first Rosalind had found it awkward calling her former teacher Maggie, even though she and Matthew had always referred to her in that way, after their flight to France. Maggie was quick to notice Rosalind's uncertainty, however, and soon put her at ease.

'You are my pupil no longer Rosalind. Please call me Maggie.'

Rosalind smiled, accepting the change in their relationship with relief. She enjoyed the older woman's company, and the natural intimacy which existed between them, although there was still one area where they both refused to go. It lay, like a submerged rock, causing an occasional awkwardness, if one of them drifted too near, but most of the time they kept well away from such danger. Maggie spoke of Matthew, as a colleague and friend, with affection and respect, but went no further, and Rosalind gave no hint that she suspected that there was any more to tell. The coolness between her and David made it unlikely that he would say anything, although Maggie worried sometimes about what would happen if the reserve between the two young people finally broke down. She had no alternative but to trust to David's discretion, and the shock at her revelation which she guessed he still felt. If they had all been characters in a novel, she would have relished the tensions between them, but in real life they didn't have quite the same appeal.

Maggie had reached the age when too much emotion made her tired, even slightly impatient, and she was determined to wear her feelings more lightly in the future. She needed her energy for other things, and was content to leave certain difficulties unresolved. It was impossible to tidy everything away, and it was probably better not to try. Age had at least taught her that. It would be enough if David and Rosalind could find some sort of peace, but as the days passed, with no obvious increase of warmth between them, that seemed more and more unlikely.

It was a week after Maggie and David had arrived in the gorge, when they were all sitting on the hotel terrace after a late breakfast, that Rosalind first mentioned Matthew's kayak. David had already been on the river several times by then, but in one of Luc's kayaks. No mention had been made of Matthew's kayak after the accident, and there was no reason to, as it would only have brought back painful speculation, best left alone. It was surprising then, even a little shocking, that Rosalind was the one to speak of it. After all it was she who had first caught sight of it, wedged under the rock face, as she directed the rescue boat, by some strange instinct towards that fateful place.

It was all the more shocking because it came up so casually in the conversation. They were talking quite light heartedly about Matthew's obsession with the river, even to the point where Rosalind said laughingly, that she always came a very poor second in his affections. Nobody took her seriously, but instead they were all relieved she could now talk about Matthew in such a relaxed way. It was at that point, as the laughter subsided, that she suddenly turned to David.

'Would you like to have a look at your father's kayak? The one he was using when he died,' she added, with a directness and brutality, which swept away any lingering smiles and laughter, and left them all feeling upset and embarrassed.

David was so taken aback he couldn't reply immediately. The colour had drained from his face, and he stared at Rosalind in bewilderment.

'Surely it was destroyed— in the accident?' he said after a few minutes.

'No,' Rosalind said bluntly. 'It's not that easy to destroy a kayak—they are usually very strong, and your father's was particularly well made. I had an identical one, but blue, not yellow. I haven't been out in it since – since that day, but they're both still in the little shed we had made for them. I'll show you if you like.'

Her tone of voice had softened as she spoke, as if she was already regretting her earlier harshness, and without giving him time to reply she stood up, ready to leave.

'Are you going now?' Luc said anxiously, sensing Rosalind was in a strange, almost combative mood.

'Why not?' she replied. 'No time like the present. Coming David?'

The young man stumbled to his feet, eager and hesitant at the same time.

Maggie laid a restraining hand on his arm.

'Take it easy, David. There's no hurry. Ros will wait.'

Maggie shot a warning look at Rosalind as she spoke, so that the younger woman reddened a little and lowered her eyes. Within minutes a happy, relaxed, scene had become fraught with unspoken emotion, and it left them all uneasy.

Rosalind and David walked in silence, Rosalind slightly ahead, leading the way. They threaded their way quickly through the tourists ambling along the river front, stopping every now and then to browse among the goods, spilling out of shop fronts onto the broad pavement. There was an angry urgency in Rosalind's walk, which stirred up the simmering resentment David still felt for his father's lover, and by the time they reached the far end of the village, they were both ready for the battle they knew was to come.

The hut, a bit like a small, garden shed, was set well back from the river on a low bank of stones, and was one of several built to house the kayaks of local residents, over the winter months.

Taking a key from her pocket, Rosalind approached the hut and undid the padlock. Light flooded into the musty darkness, as Rosalind propped open the door with a large stone, and David followed her inside. There were no windows in the shed and it took them a moment or two to adjust to the gloom.

Two, long, narrow, shapes crouched under a large sheet of canvas, which Rosalind hastily pulled back to reveal the kayaks, lying side by side, like figures on some ancient tomb.

'There are some marks on your father's kayak where it was caught under the rock, but otherwise it's in perfect condition,' Rosalind said quietly, a slight catch in her voice, as if she had a cold coming.

David knelt down beside his father's kayak, and laid a hand on its curved side. A shudder passed through him, and his shoulders shook with the sobs he could no longer suppress.

Rosalind felt her own heart become cold, and small, and heavy, inside her chest, and she struggled to breathe. The silence between them seemed loaded with all the pain they couldn't express, as each waited with a childlike stubbornness, for the other to weaken.

David was the first to blink. His need to know was too great to hold out any longer.

'Why did he go on the river that day? Why didn't you stop him?'

His cry came, like a terrible echo of her own agony, but her words were stilted and angry, as if she had no understanding of his pain.

' He didn't tell me he was going. He deceived me. It was his own fault. He knew the dangers as well as anyone. He— he made his death happen—no one else. I would have stopped him if I could, but I never got the chance. Surely you believe that? Your father was a fool, David, a rash, selfish, fool and –,' she hesitated, 'I hate him for that.'

'How dare you!'

David was on his feet, his face white and taut with anger, his fists clenched tight at his sides.

'How dare you speak of my father like that! You had him—his love—for all those years and you talk of hate. If you really want to know what hate feels like ask me.'

David thumped his chest again and again with a clenched fist, as if hammering the words, like nails, into his own heart.

'I have hated you so much and for so long for taking him away from me, but I always hoped that one day you would die, and he would come and find me. Now he's made that impossible, and I hate him too. I'm a fool, Rosalind, just like my father, for dreaming that things could be different. They can't be. They won't be. This is how it is.'

The despair in David's last few words reminded Rosalind so strongly of Matthew, in his bleaker moments, that she stretched out her hand towards him in a tentative gesture of truce. For a moment it seemed as if David would take her outstretched hand, but instead he turned away, and left the shed without another word.

It was almost half an hour before Rosalind felt able to follow him. Dazed and upset, she kicked the stone away and pushed the door to behind her. The key was still in the padlock but she gave it no thought. There was nothing left to protect.

They had all planned to have a meal as usual in the hotel that evening, but Rosalind couldn't face it. She sent a message to Luc, saying she had a migraine and was having an early night. David would know why she wasn't there. It was up to him what he said to the others.

The temperature had risen steadily over the previous few

days, and the evening was hot and close. Rosalind made herself a sandwich soon after seven but couldn't finish it. Her appetite had gone as well as her ability to concentrate. She had tried to work on a short story she was anxious to finish, but her mind felt empty of ideas and words, and she gave up in disgust. Pacing restlessly round the flat, she went over the conversation with David, coming back again and again to his last words, 'This is how it is,' with a heavy heart. The anger had gone, but had left behind an aching sadness, which wore her down. When the doorbell rang it was quite a relief, although she wasn't expecting anyone.

Glancing at her watch, as she went to open the door, she saw it was nearly nine o'clock, and already completely dark outside.

Maggie was on the doorstep, and the look of anxiety on her face sent a thrill of alarm through Rosalind.

'What's the matter? Is something wrong?' Her words were quick and urgent as she stepped back to let Maggie in.

'It's David. He didn't turn up for the meal this evening. We can't find him anywhere, and wondered whether he had come here. Luc's very busy in the hotel so I said I would pop up and see. Hope you don't mind.'

A terrible panic seized Rosalind. It was all happening again, and although she felt powerless to stop it, she had to try.

'He will have gone on the river. We must get down there now.'

She pushed Maggie back towards the door and grabbed her keys and phone from her bag.

'I'll ring Luc on the way. He may have to call the rescue boat.'

Maggie, swept along by Rosalind's calm desperation, did as she was told. She realised at once what she had done and it filled her with horror. For Rosalind, it wasn't David who was missing but Matthew. The nightmare had begun again.

Maggie could hardly keep up with Rosalind as they ran through the narrow streets, finding it hard to keep their footing on the slippery stones, polished to a high gloss by the feet of countless tourists.

'Slow down a bit,' Maggie gasped, as they reached the church and prepared to cross the road. 'Where are we going exactly?'

'To the hut, to see if the kayak has gone,' Rosalind shouted back, as she darted across the road. 'He's a fool like his father. He admitted it.'

Approaching the hut, there was no sign of anyone on the narrow, stony, beach, but the door was open, and swinging gently in the evening breeze. There was a cry of dismay from Rosalind, and as Maggie joined her at the door of the hut, they both stared helplessly at the canvas sheet, pulled carelessly aside, and the empty space where the kayak should have been.

Rosalind spoke in a whisper and Maggie strained to hear her.

'Please tell me it's not true, Maggie. It can't happen again.'

'It won't,' Maggie replied bravely. 'Nothing happens twice, not in exactly the same way.'

She put an arm round Rosalind to add more comfort to her words, and as she did so, there was a shout from the river, and the sound of a kayak beaching.

'It's David,' Maggie cried, 'it's David, Rosalind. He's back.'

Her words got no response. Rosalind had already left her side, and was running towards the dark shape pulling the kayak further out of the water. The figure, straightening up, turned to meet her, as she flung herself into his arms, sobbing with angry joy and beating his chest with her fists.

Afterword

David and Maggie were to fly home on the first Monday in July, and on the Sunday, their last day, Maggie suggested they all walk up to the Hermitage. Ever since reading Rosalind's novella she had been intrigued and moved by the story of the young princess who had found both healing and sanctuary in the gorge. It was a tale of loss and redemption, which seemed to find an echo, a reflection, in all their lives, and could perhaps also bring them the final healing each of them craved.

Rosalind was pleased that her story of the Saint had caught Maggie's imagination, and she felt a sudden surge of excitement at the thought of showing her beloved mentor the site of the original cave, now incorporated into the tiny chapel of The Hermitage.

'It's a very special place', she said quietly to Maggie when she mentioned the walk. 'I think you will like it. It has an atmosphere but –'.

She didn't say anymore because she couldn't. The effect the place had on her was too elusive to describe.

'I'm sure I will,' Maggie replied. 'In some ways I feel I have already been there,' she added after a moment or two. 'That atmosphere—it's in the book—and more than a hint of it.'

Rosalind smiled.

'I wanted something to come through. I wasn't sure it had.'

'Oh yes,' Maggie said decisively. 'Something comes through all right. I'd like David to feel it too. He isn't at peace yet. It could help.'

'We should go when it's cooler,' Rosalind said, casting an anxious glance at Maggie. 'It's a tough climb.'

They were sitting on the hotel terrace, waiting for David to join them for lunch, and the sun was very hot, even through the shifting shade of the vine, which petered out just above their table. Luc was working and couldn't join them, but would be free later in the afternoon.

Since the moment by the river, nearly three days ago, the closeness between the two women had regained something of its former intensity, and they both felt a quiet sadness at the prospect of their imminent separation. It had taken time to find the old feelings, but now restored, they both felt reluctant to let them go. Maggie had already suggested that Rosalind should return to England for a visit, if not to stay, but Rosalind had shook her head, avoiding Maggie's gaze.

'I've thought about it, but I don't think I can. Not while he's –,' she paused, afraid that her words would sound faintly ridiculous, even to Maggie.

'Not while he's still here,' Maggie added, without a trace of mockery in her voice.

'I understand.'

When the idea of the walk to The Hermitage was put to David, he wasn't keen. He had been looking forward to a last evening on the river, and by the time they returned it would be too late to take the kayak out. Maggie sensed his reluctance and didn't press him, but he could see the look of disappointment on Rosalind's face, and he blushed guiltily. It was Luc who came to the rescue.

'You're not flying until tomorrow evening. You could go on the river very early in the morning. Say your farewells then. It's so quiet at that time, better than the evening.'

David smiled gratefully.

'Yes. You're right. I'll do that. Thanks, Luc.'

He was relieved that he wouldn't have to upset Maggie and Rosalind, particularly Rosalind. Their reconciliation had been hard won, and he didn't want to do anything at the last minute to jeopardise it.

They were to meet at Rosalind's flat at 6 pm, and in the meantime David and Maggie returned to their rooms to pack, and Rosalind helped Luc clear up after lunch, and prepare the tables for the evening.

Rosalind had done the walk up to The Hermitage so many times before, but it had never lost its appeal. It always left the climber with aching limbs and little breath, but the rewards were worth it. From every station of the cross, and there were fourteen of them, the view of the village and gorge changed so dramatically that the intrepid climber saw the scene afresh each time. With every step, the village retreated further into the rock face, until its complete shape could be seen, nestling in the embrace of rock and river.

Rosalind led the way, and Luc brought up the rear. She set a steady pace, but allowed plenty of time at each station for them all to recover. Maggie was immediately behind her, and she was acutely aware of the older woman's laboured breathing, as they approached each new resting place.

When they reached the seventh station, they rested for a

little longer than usual. They were half way up, and the view was already so fine, that Maggie and David fell silent in their wonder. The sun had abandoned the depths of the gorge and was retreating up the rock face, casting most of the village into shadow, apart from the school and the remains of the old abbey, which still caught its last rays. No sound reached them of the lively crowds, still thronging the narrow streets, and the only signs of modern life were the tiny cars, edging their way down the far side of the gorge, their lights like fireflies, flitting to and fro in the gathering dusk.

The years fell away, and the ancient village reasserted itself, as seen by the princess at the end of her wanderings. Gazing at the timeless scene, Maggie too felt the pull of the old story, which Rosalind had brought so vividly to life in her book, and she turned eagerly towards her former pupil to share her delight. Rosalind, however, seemed lost in her own thoughts, and was looking back down the path they had just climbed, as if she half expected someone to emerge from the dying light, and join them on their journey. But there was no movement on the path below, just an occasional griffon vulture, drifting lazily on a warm current of air, as it searched the rocks for likely prey, its wing tips brushing the tops of the taller bushes, as it rose and fell in its sinister pursuit.

'I think we should get a move on,' Luc said, after they had rested for almost ten minutes. The light is going fast and we don't want to make the descent in the dark.'

'Yes, you're right,' Rosalind replied briskly, jolted out of her own reverie, by Luc's warning.

For the second part of the climb, Luc took the lead, as there were some particularly steep and difficult stretches to negotiate, where the track split in two, and his familiarity with the path, which he had scampered up so often as a boy, made it easy for him to choose the best route, where the footing was firm, and the way not too overgrown.

They walked in silence, conserving their energy, as they struggled up high steps, cut out of the rock itself, their breath coming in short gasps, and their hands reaching out for a nearby bush to steady themselves. Maggie and Rosalind fell a little way behind the two men, who, at one point, disappeared completely from view. Rosalind, who was now last, was reluctant to hurry Maggie whom she could tell was finding the second part of the climb particularly arduous.

'Take your time', she said gently, as Maggie came to a halt at the foot of a steep flight of rough steps which led directly up to the twelfth station. 'We're nearly there. Another ten minutes or so and you can have a proper rest.'

Maggie turned and smiled at Rosalind.

'You're very kind. An old soul, as an Indian once said. Matthew was very lucky.'

Rosalind felt a lump rise in her throat.

'I'm so sorry for what we put you through,' she whispered to Maggie, who had turned back to tackle the steps. 'Can you forgive us?'

Maggie did not reply until they reached the top of the steps. Round the corner, they could hear the men talking, as they waited for them at the twelfth station, their voices full of laughter in the warm, evening, air.

'There's nothing to forgive—not anymore,' she said, her voice a little tremulous as she brushed Rosalind's cheek gently with the back of her hand. 'Remember, I need forgiveness too. For that night –,' she paused, 'the one I stole from you. Can you manage that?'

Rosalind nodded, and bent her head to hide the tears. Her heart was full, but the pain had gone.

* * *

Like a blessing they hadn't expected, The Hermitage was still in the full sun when they reached it. The shadows were fast approaching, but for the moment they had beaten them.

Excited and proud, Rosalind showed her friends the tiny chapel built over and out from the deep cave where, according to legend, the Saint had lived out her last days, centuries before. Then she led them round a high shoulder of rock to the place of the spring, where the healing waters were said to have cured the princess of the terrible curse of leprosy. Nothing remained but a shallow depression in the shelf of rock, half filled with stagnant rainwater, and a strange outline in the smooth stone, which legend claimed to be the shape of the saint's body, impressed on the rock for ever.

Breathless, with an emotion she could hardly contain, Rosalind told the story again, just as she had heard it when she first came to the village, so many years before. Every now and then she would look up and catch Luc's eye, and he would nod his approval of her telling.

Maggie was visibly moved, and even David seemed entranced. The story wove its magic so swiftly, and gathered them all in, as if they too were part of its suffering and healing. The ghosts had departed and the place was free, but as the story drew to a close, something still remained in the hearts of those who lived on.

Standing with David, by the low wall which bordered the grassy area just in front of The Hermitage, Rosalind looked down towards the river, lost now in the evening shadows. Matthew had died in that darkness, but his son was standing next to her.

Loved but unseen, the river flowed on, and all was as it should be.

Printed in Great
Britain
by Amazon